Books by Jay Erickson

The Blood Wizard Chronicles-

Pariah
Recreant

I0457068

Blood Wizard Chronicles Novellas-

Stormwind
Dark Consort
Pononga

Role-Playing Game Adventures

The Wild Tide

A BLOOD WIZARD CHRONICLES NOVELLA:

BARROW of LIES

By: Jay Erickson

HALSBREN
PUBLISHING, LLC

BARROW OF LIES

Edited by Kathleen LaSelle
Cover art by Jay Erickson

THE PURVEYOR

Edited by Vicki Beaver of Obatron Productions
Spriggan Concept Art by Ashley Erickson of HardShellArt
Interior Design by Jay Erickson

Published By: Halsbren Publishing LLC. *La Porte, IN. 46350*
ISBN: 978-1-942958-14-7
Made in the United States of America.

DEDICATION

To everyone who has given me so much enthusiasm and encouragement over the last three years to continue to expand the ever growing world of Kuldarr. This dedication is for you. Thank you all.

-Jay Erickson

~ ~ ~

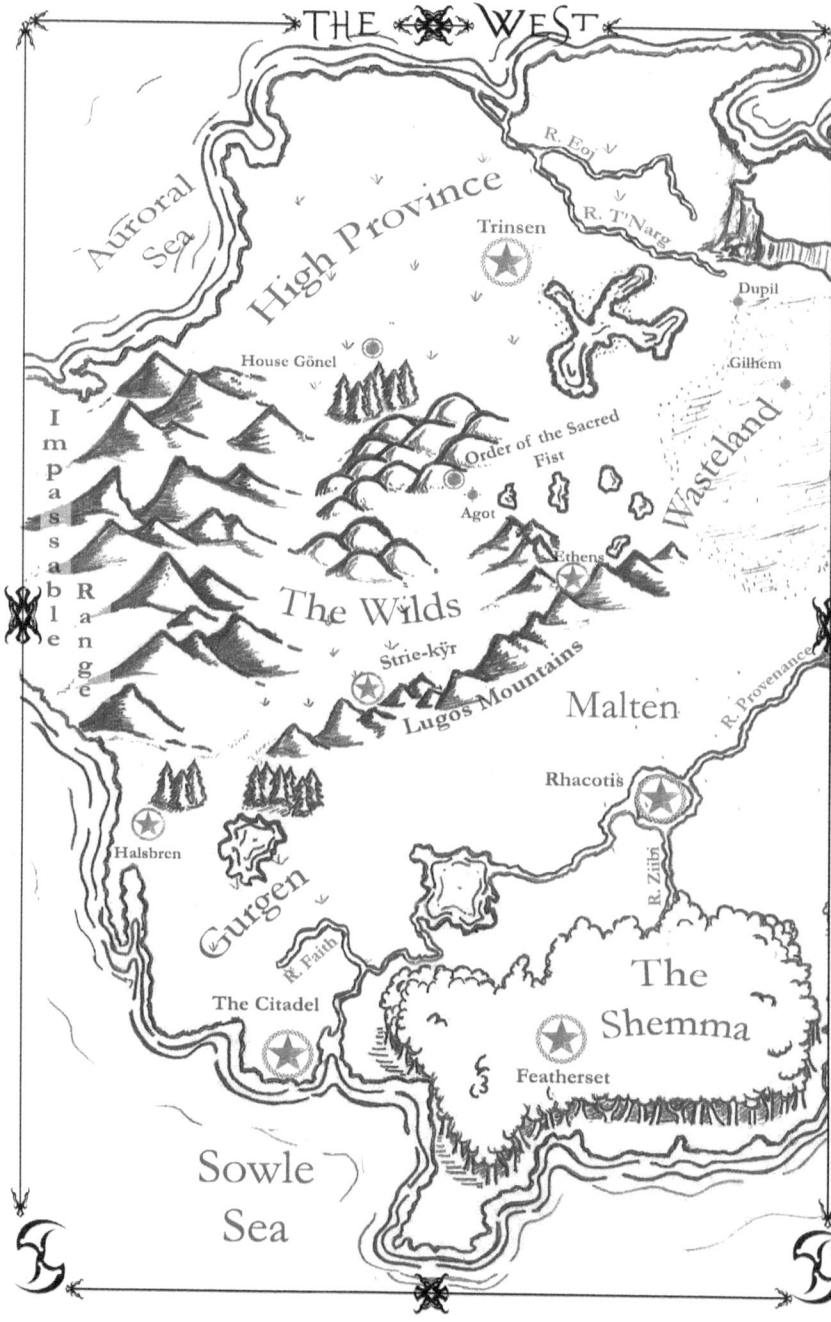

THE ✦ WEST

Auroral Sea

High Province

R. Eoi

R. T'Narg

Trinsen

Dupil

Gilhem

House Gönel

Order of the Sacred Fist

Agot

Wasteland

Impassable Range

Ethens

The Wilds

Strie-kÿr

Lugos Mountains

Malten

R. Provenance

Rhacotis

R. Ziibi

Halsbren

Gurgen

The Shemma

R. Faith

The Citadel

Featherset

Sowle Sea

TABLE OF CONTENTS

BARROW OF LIES
Prelude
The Promotion
Simonis
Authority
Wheel
Manor
Haunt
The Scene
The Glyph
Only Human
Graveyard
Deception
Reveal
Master Key
Endgame
Epilogue

Bonus Materials:

THE PURVEYOR

STORMWIND: Sample Chapter

FORWARD

When Stormwind debuted in 2015, I wrote it in the hopes of introducing readers to my brand of storytelling, and to seque the reader toward the novel, Pariah, something that I thought was my true tale to be told. Stormwind was intended to be a single story in the grand scheme of the Kuldarr Universe, nothing more. Things don't always go as one would think though...

Within the first few months of its tandem release with Pariah, the Stormwind tale drew audiences to it in a way I did not expect. They were riveted to the hero, Stormwind, of course, but it was the secondary characters that so many talked about. Fans and friends alike wanted to know about the histories of Aodhfin Bray and Carmella Daz. History that I had not given too much thought into, because I never intended for them to exist past that introductory tale. The readers wanted to know more about them. More about the nature of Purists. What the Jasian Enclave represented? Quite simply - they wanted more Stormwind.

So in celebration of the three year anniversary of Stormwind, and his lasting presence on the minds of the readers, Halsbren Publishing LLC is proud to release Barrow of Lies.

Within these pages, is a prequel novella that truly introduces the Purist Aodhfin Bray, and showcases what a unique character he is in this universe.

Also included is the short story, The Purveyor. It is a tale about an exactor named Rhall who must track down a rogue sorcerer that is murdering innocent children using summoned creatures known as Ursers. What Rhall unveils however, changes everything. This story is the last piece of the puzzle locked in place, and sets the stage for the events that transpire within Stormwind. It is just a little bit extra knowledge of this growing universe, and my way of saying a very special thank you to you, the fans.

So I hope you enjoy Barrow of Lies, and thank you for taking a chance and stepping into my universe. Kuldarr always has room for more…

-Jay Erickson
Author

4848 E.o.E

**SEVEN WINTERS PRIOR TO THE EVENTS
OF STORMWIND**

PRELUDE

Bray couldn't move.

Fear, oppressive and heavy, like water-laden armor, weighed upon him. A set of menacing eyes looked at him, victorious. They wracked his body with terror as they came closer. Eyes that burned with an unholy green flame.

Bray wanted to raise his shield in defense. He wanted to pray to the Maker for his chosen deity's courage and blessings. He wanted to run. But he couldn't.

Paralyzed, and with an all-consuming dread, he watched, helpless, as it drifted towards him. A revolting, distorted head, suspended from insect-like wings. Around its ominous gaze was a crown of writhing tentacles all capped with wicked, barbed spines. Bray could see a pus-like fluid oozing from each of the dozen or so spurs.

The monster's mouth opened. He heard a loud pop and watched in disbelief as its jaws distended wide enough that it could enclose its maw completely around his own head. Jagged teeth slavered at the impending kill, and Aodhfin Bray knew without a doubt that he was doomed.

THE PROMOTION

72 hours earlier...

Sea spray misted his face, a squall of salty droplets that filled his nostrils and left a bitter taste on his tongue. He looked out across the deep blue waters spread out before him. Just at the edge of the horizon, he could make out the first signs of humanity since he, Aodhfin Bray, left the massive metropolis of the Citadel, heart of the Jasian Enclave.

Three weeks.

It had taken them three weeks. From initial notification to now, arriving just outside of the port town of Sentinel's Barrow had been twenty-one days. So much could happen in three weeks' time. What did they truly expect him to do?

Aodhfin's fingers brushed across the foreign locket at his neck. It was odd there. He wasn't used to wearing the bauble. He found it comforting though, and helpful in thinking, as he was doing now.

Twenty-one days.

Aodhfin Bray had been recently 'promoted'. It had not been one earned through meritorious service, but through blood; a field promotion.

A field promotion was not an odd thing for his chosen vocation of purist. He was a holy warrior for the church of the Maker, and bound to the doctrines of the Jasian Enclave. As such, violence was his way of life. He lived by conflict, and he knew he would one day die by it, as had happened to his commander.

What was odd, however, was that the attackers that he had fought had managed to infiltrate the Citadel itself. Usually all skirmishes with the Wilders, barbarians from the north, happened on the outer borders of the nation. The Citadel was nowhere near the conflict areas. It was located deep within Gurgen, far to the south against the deep waters of the Sowle Sea.

It was a bastion to the faithful. Its monolithic walls were supposed to keep all dangers out, and protect the pious within. For the Wilders to have managed to sneak within those massive hallowed walls... it was hard to fathom.

They had remained out of sight for weeks, eluding all patrols, civilizations, and even merchants. Well-organized and efficient, when they finally breached the Citadel walls, they had all the advantages. They might have been able to steal anything, or even kill one of the most powerful people in the world.

Each Wilder had known it was likely a suicide mission. Once within the Citadel it was a death sentence. Therefore, if they were going to track down and eliminate anyone within the religious conurbation it should be someone whose death would have been the most impactful and destructive to the religious imperium.

Instead, they sought to assassinate a woman. To Aodhfin this was vexing: Proffering to give up their own lives to kill someone of very little tactical merit.

While Jasia, martyr of the Maker, and his chosen daughter, was the cornerstone of their faith, no woman held any power within the Enclave. Not militarily, nor politically.

They had many sisters who led services and assisted in prayers. Women supplied themselves to trades of healing and alchemy, nursing and tradecraft. Yet none was allowed a position of any such significance that infiltrating one of the most heavily-fortified bastions in the world to kill her made any kind of sense. Yet they had done it anyway, and when questioned why, they had only uttered a single word.

Ambrosia.

Aodhfin did not know who or what Ambrosia was. No one in the Enclave did. The Wilders had taken this one and only chance to breach the Citadel's defenses, and they wasted it on a ghost.

The purists tracked and cornered the insurgents. Instead of learning more about Ambrosia, the Wilders fought and died, taking their knowledge of this Ambrosia to their graves.

It was no victory for Aodhfin. His commander and close friend, Ser Barodin Simonis, had been the first to fall at the assassins' skilled hands. Aodhfin took command of his unit, and with the loss of only two more purists he had eliminated the Wilders.

Three good men had died, and Aodhfin would likely never know why. Why these insurgents had risked everything, and killed Aodhfin Bray's brothers-at-arms for a single word.

Now, as the salty froth washed against his face once more, he thought of what he was going to say to Bishop Simonis when he saw him. His son was dead, slain within walls thought to be impenetrable. Yet more disturbing was that it had come at the most unfortunate time. Someone had contacted the Citadel for help within Sentinel's Barrow.

Of course, Aodhfin would come to their aide. It was all he could do. He dropped his hand from the locket and looked back to the stern of the ship. As part of his new role as purist commander, they had assigned him two exactors for the tasking.

Mercenaries.

Aodhfin felt his lip curl in disgust. He would have rather traveled with his unit, but Adjutant Daz had not thought it prudent. Though he was going to report the death of a devout purist to the family, the real reason he was here was to look into a murder, and possibly, if the missive he had received was correct, a haunting.

For that, he needed an exactor, a contractor that worked for the Jasian Enclave, but had no religious or political affiliation to it. The church exploited a loophole so that it may use sorcerers within its ranks. This way they still maintained abstinence from such magics itself, while not becoming victims from it. It was also a fortunate coincidence, because if the exactor was found doing something heretical, the church could 'wash their hands of it' and claim no connection.

The Enclave only permitted the healing and cleansing magic of **Creation** to be used while bearing the will of the religious nation-state. They were never allowed to bend creation for avarice, ever. However, an outside source, hired for a purpose, such as an exactor... well, that was a grey area.

Aodhfin did not care for the use of magic. He trusted in only three things: his faith in the Maker, the strength of his shield, and the quality of his skills to see him through. Relying on such an extraneous ability like magic seemed foolhardy. Why wield something that imparts a sacrifice on the user? Why weaken yourself on the field of battle and make yourself easy prey to an arrow or axe? Why control something that equally controls you?

He saw the sorcerer now, losing his last meal once more over the side of the vessel. Bray shook his head at the incompetent exactor. Perhaps the sorcerer should have learned a spell of stomach tranquility?

This 'magic man' was a High Elf from Trinsen, capital of the High Province, a nation so far north it was past even the Wilds. Aodhfin had never been there. Most of his life he had spent in Gurgen. Only when he became a purist had he started to see pieces of the world around him.

The Elf's name was Lotul Varthstone, and he claimed he was from a family of esteemed sorcerers.

He touted that sorcery had been in his family for the last five millennia. Ever since the beginning of the Sixth Era; The Era of Enlightenment.

Aodhfin thought Lotul was an idiot. If this Varthstone was so good at using creation, then why was he so sick every day on the ship? Why couldn't he conjure sea legs?

Still, he knew that Lotul had other uses. Being a High Elf, or Goldhym, as they referred to themselves, afforded him sway with the other Elves that were within Sentinel's Barrow.

The port town was unique within Gurgen. It was the only town that supported an equal amount of humans, and Elves. Oddly enough, they had co-mingled harmoniously for many winters. At least until now...

The use of Lotul may sway some of the locals in his favor. Purists, though adored by many within Gurgen's borders, were also feared. They acted in the name of the Maker, and as such, operated as judge, jury, and executioner. This gave them a 'power' that left many uncomfortable. Luckily, purists were men of the Maker, and so they never abused such power, Aodhfin included.

Aodhfin also knew that Lotul had... features... that would enable him to associate well with the gentler side of the species. Many women considered his tall height, long and straight golden hair, pale skin, and smooth face attractive. The Elf also had a unique way of looking at the fairer gender with his hazel eyes. When he did, it seemed to make every woman he encountered blush and bat her lashes at him.

Aodhfin, himself, had no such need for frivolities. He knew his hooded blue eyes, pronounced brow, and strong set jaw were often found unappealing by the opposite sex. Had he not been raised in the confines of the Citadel it might have meant something, but as it stood, his facial traits mattered little to him. A purist lived a life for the Maker. He did not spend it sowing his oats with every willing participant he found. As dictated by the Jasian Enclave, a wife was selected for him by his family, or the Church.

Such a woman waited for him back at the Citadel now. One of the loveliest and most gifted creatures he ever had the luxury of meeting. She had soft dark hair that seemed impossible to control, and eyes the color of chocolate. She was fifteen winters old, and soon, on her sixteenth she would be his. The Maker smiled upon him for granting such a union. Soon they would be wed, and a proper, bountiful family would blossom in its wake.

Until that time, he would remain pure of heart and of body. He hadn't seen her in over a winter now. Not that it meant much. Often purists were gone for long periods. She had his heart, and that was all that mattered. After all, he had a job to do in the Maker's name.

He shook the thought of his lovely fiancée from his mind and called Lotul down from the stern. The pale Elf looked at him forlornly and shambled down the stairs, holding the side rail for dear life as the ship pitched up and down. Aodhfin thought the Elf looked green.

"Where is Sange?" he barked at the seasick Elf.

The sorcerer managed a weak shrug. "I'm not that bison's keeper. Find her yourself."

Aodhfin scowled at the pompous Elf, though he couldn't dispute his comparison of the large muscular woman with such a strong animal.

Sange was a massive and stout woman that stood taller than most men. She was young, like he, at only eighteen winters old. Her arms were thick with hard muscles, and she had a barrel of a chest, with breasts so small they might as well not exist. She wore simple leathers over her heavily muscled body, and favored a lumber axe as her weapon of choice. Were it not for the misleadingly soft round features of her face, with her large doe brown eyes, a button nose, and curvaceous lips, she could easily be mistaken for a man.

When Aodhfin had first been introduced to Sange, he thought that she was a Wilder. Yet she had grown up protected within the borders of Gurgen, in a small lumber-town on the edge of the Shemma Great Woods. He knew it explained the leathers and why she favored an axe, but it did little to answer her size.

Wilders were known to be upwards of seven feet tall, and she had to be almost that tall, perhaps a stone shorter. The purist had no doubt there was Wilder ancestry there, but if the Enclave accepted it, and she wasn't against fighting the northern hordes, then he too had no objection.

Besides, she favored skill and the strength of her arm over the powers of the mind. That was something she and Aodhfin agreed on.

Just as he was about to admonish the annoying sorcerer, Aodhfin heard a crash from below, followed by raucous laughter. Moments later the hatch flew open, and the large frame of Sange came climbing out, her trademark lumber axe tethered to her back. Blood trickled from her nose, but she wore a broad grin on her small shapely mouth.

Two more of the deck hands followed afterwards, each looking worse for the wear. Blood matted their hair, and scuffs marked their disheveled clothing. Already one of them had a swollen and darkening eye.

"Man, ye guys have some weird customs," the big woman's deceptively sweet voice intoned as she wrapped both of them in a bear hug once they were on deck.

"Ye were good fer da crew, Sange," black eye said. "Ye eva wanna sail, ye come back!"

Sange nodded at them and then looked to Aodhfin. "I hear ye was lookin' fer me, Ser."

Aodhfin nodded. Though she was an exactor, she knew rank and station and afforded it to him. He appreciated that, considering that Varthstone knew no such respect. They were all here, and after three weeks of waiting, the time was upon him.

His eyes drifted once more to the green and brown mass that was now growing closer with every bob of the prow. The spires of the Enclave were in sight. Soon he would be ashore, and he would have to face Bishop Simonis and inform him of the fate of his son.

SIMONIS

Bishop Simonis was far from an imposing man. Standing almost a head shorter than Aodhfin Bray and stooped with the beginnings of a man entering his twilight winters, the pudgy holy man looked more like a settled sack of potatoes then the Enclave's resident leader.

Thin grey hair combed over a baldpate and jowls that resembled the neck of a chicken completed his look. His son had looked nothing like the man before him, and Aodhfin only hoped that he had gotten much of his looks from his mother.

Simonis' jowls wavered as he shook his head and spoke. "No," he said, "I did not request any purists. The Enclave is mistaken. Your time was wasted."

He dismissed Bray without a single glance from his droopy hazel eyes and sat back into his plush chair. "Now if you will excuse me, Purist Grey, I am a busy man."

"Bray," Aodhfin countered, not letting the man get to him. "I was told about a murder that needed solving, though. Adjutant Daz was rather insistent."

Simonis dismissed his comment with a wave of his hand. "Daz," he harrumphed. "That old coot thinks we can't do our job here well enough! We may not have purists stationed here at the Burrow, but we have an adjutant! Hells, we had two!"

"Two?"

Simonis nodded. "Man who was murdered was retired and living his last winters in peace. Good enough man, Vey Gallach was. It's a loss, truly."

"An adjutant was murdered and you feel that I'm not needed here?" Bray remarked, incredulous.

Simonis smiled condescendingly. "Contrary to what you believe young man, we are fully capable of solving crimes without purists, you know."

"He was an adjutant!"

"Retired," Simonis reiterated. "Besides, it was a cut-and-dried case. His wife, Esme, murdered him. She was found at the scene, weapon in hand. She had stabbed him multiple times. Blood coated her hands and the murder weapon. It was upon her body, and even sprayed the walls! Adjutant Murrough was the first responder. So, it was pretty clear. She killed her husband in a crime of passion."

"I see," Aodhfin said, tight-lipped. "So she's imprisoned then? I would much like to speak to her myself."

"That is not possible," Simonis retorted. "She killed an ex-adjutant. There's only one response for that, my boy, and you know that."

"What's he mean by that?" Sange asked from behind Bray.

"The rules for women are very clear," Simonis said sternly. "She murdered a man of the Maker in cold blood. She cast her own soul to the Defiler when she did so. The only pardon from such an act is to brighten her spirit once more in the hopes that the Maker will see something worth saving that we mere mortals cannot."

"What in the hells is that supposed to mean?" Varthstone asked, as tactless as ever.

"It means absolution through fire," Bray answered.

He looked at both Sange and Varthstone, who stared at him, confused.

"Esme is dead," he told them. "She was burned alive."

AUTHORITY

"What the hells is wrong with ye people!" Sange yelled at Simonis.

"Purist, control your exactors," Simonis replied calmly, not even addressing Sange.

Aodhfin raised his hand to silence Sange. Her eyes went wide with incredulousness. He ignored it, and spoke to the Bishop. "I would like to make inquiries, if I may?"

"Why?" Simonis asked, a shadow crossing over his features.

"As a purist assigned here by the Enclave, it is my responsibility to report that justice was dealt accurately. I just need to confer with your people and see the crime scene, and I will be out of your way."

Simonis nodded. "I can understand that," he answered, his turkey-neck wobbling. "Adjutant Murrough is at the garrison. I would recommend speaking with him first."

Bray nodded as well. "And who is the mortician responsible for handling the deceased?"

"Fem Fonzil."

"Fonzil is a High Elf surname?" Varthstone inquired.

The Bishop nodded. "It's not uncommon. You will find an equal mix of Elves and humans here, exactor."

"Did Ser Fonzil exhume both bodies?" Bray asked.

Simonis nodded.

"Where did the crime take place?"

Simonis looked out his window to the north. "Gallach Manor. Adjutant Murrough can direct you, or he can assign some of our local militia to assist you. Just don't go in there alone."

"Why?"

Simonis shifted in his lush chair uncomfortably. "Well, ever since Gallach died, the manor has been unwelcoming of people."

"Unwelcomin'?" Sange asked.

"It's haunted," Varthstone replied and then pointed a thumb at himself. "That's why I'm here."

Simonis scrutinized the Elf, "How did you…," his eyes snapped open wide. "Daria!"

He spat the name so quickly that Aodhfin almost missed it. "Who's Daria?"

Simonis waved his hand dismissively. "We're done here. If you want any more questions answered, I suggest you speak with Adjutant Murrough. I'm a very busy man."

"Who is Daria?" Bray repeated. He was beginning to grow concerned. Simonis was acting very strangely.

The Bishop growled at him. "Get out!" he yelled, "Or I'll have you removed! I am still in charge here, and an upstart purist and his team of thugs will not patronize me! I gave you authorization to speak to the others. You want answers, get it from them."

Aodhfin eyed the Bishop curiously as the man turned the color of a plum in his fury. Then he nodded.

"Let's go," he told the Exactors.

He bowed once to the Bishop. "Ser." Bray then extricated himself from the man's quarters. He would tell Simonis about his son's death later; right now he had a murder to solve.

~ ~ ~

"Animals," Sange muttered as they walked down the cobblestone path from the rectory of the Jasian

Enclave and to the garrison where they hoped to find Adjutant Murrough.

"It is law," Bray answered. "She murdered a man of the cloth and darkened her soul. The only way to gain freedom from such a mar is to lighten it."

"They set er' on fire," Sange said through gritted teeth. "Burburic."

"I think what you meant to say was 'barbaric'," Lotul responded. "But, yes I agree."

"It is law," Bray said again simply.

"Would they burn a man alive if he had murdered a sister?" Varthstone asked.

Bray didn't answer.

As they approached the flat one-story structure of crème colored stone, Bray knew he was at the right spot. He had seen dozens of them, growing up in a family of purists. The outside of the garrison was plain, having no decorative crenellations or encrustations of any kind. Purists were men who lived without need for extravagance.

Square windows dotted the otherwise nondescript building, and a thick oak door was the only obvious entrance.

Before Aodhfin could reach for the door, it suddenly flew open. There in the doorway was an older man, perhaps in his late forties to early fifties. He was lean, with a sharp hooked nose, thin lips, and piercing blue eyes. Brown hair cascaded down around his shoulders and was covered by a feathered cap. On his chest, he wore the blue tabard embedded with a white circumpunct in the middle. The tabard was standard garb of the purist. Or in this case, an adjutant.

"Ser Murrough?" Bray asked.

The man raised an eyebrow. "And who are you, young man?"

Bray bowed. "Ser, my name is Aodhfin Bray, Purist of the Jasian Enclave, sent from Adjutant Daz to investigate the murder of Adjutant Gallach."

Bray could feel Murrough's scrutinizing gaze upon him. "The murder has been solved. Why would the Citadel send anyone?"

Bray shrugged, "That is what I am trying to find out as well, Ser."

Aodhfin studied the adjutant as the man looked over his shoulder to Sange and Varthstone behind him. "They issued you exactors, not additional purists?"

Aodhfin nodded, "Yes, ser."

"Well you will find few answers, I'm afraid. Esme was found guilty immediately and put to pyre." Murrough said as he moved around the young purist. Aodhfin fell into step beside him.

"So Bishop Simonis has informed me."

"Then there you have it," the adjutant said.

"I was wondering if I could ask you a few questions at least, so I can report back to the Citadel that justice was dispensed."

The adjutant didn't look at him as they walked. "Of course, purist."

"You were the first responder, correct?"

Murrough nodded at him. "Yes, I heard the screams of an argument and I went to investigate. My manor is across from theirs, you see."

"I see," Bray answered. "Did they argue often?"

"As much as any couple wedded to each other for so long. They wanted to kill each other daily."

Bray stopped walking.

Murrough turned to him smiling. "Sorry, poor humor. I jest," he shrugged. "They did fight some, yes. Nothing like I had heard that night though. Gallach was angry. He sounded loud and aggressive."

"Coulda she 'ave been defendin' herself?" Sange asked.

Murrough eyed her darkly. "Loud and aggressive does not mean violent," he snapped. "Vey Gallach was a good man. He did much for Sentinel's Barrow, and for the Enclave. He devoted winters of his life to countless crusades before becoming an adjutant and then settling down in this little port town. He was a hero."

"We did not mean to presume otherwise," Bray said as he scowled at Sange.

Murrough nodded. "It is a very sore subject for us," the man admitted. "We very much loved Esme, and Vey. Their deaths have impacted us all."

"Were you friends with Gallach?"

"I was there often."

"And you never saw any signs of malice between either of them?"

The Adjutant shook his head no. "Purists are above such things, remember?"

Bray nodded.

Murrough looked out over the horizon and the purist followed the man's gaze. In the distance, he saw a young woman, near his age, tending a garden. She had long black hair that shimmered in the sunlight, but her back was to them.

"Is there anything else, purist?" Murrough asked, impatient.

"One more question," Aodhfin said. "Who is Daria?"

Murrough's face scrunched in either disgust or anger, Aodhfin wasn't sure. He spat on the ground. "Her name is Daria Gallach.

"Gallach?" Bray asked.

"By birth she's Vey and Esme's daughter."

WHEEL

"What do you mean, by birth?" Bray asked. Murrough, now impatient to move on, looked Bray in the eyes. "She has disavowed the Maker, and no longer considers herself one of his children. She's a pagan and a heretic now."

Aodhfin was shocked. He had never heard of such a thing, at least not from a child of an adjutant. Once in a family as committed to the Maker as purists and adjutants were, always committed.

"Who does she worship now?" Sange asked behind him, unmoved by the adjutant's words.

"Non-committal as far as I know, though I couldn't really care less," he said dismissively. "Now really purist, I have things to do."

Bray nodded. "I understand," he answered with a bow of his head. "Thank you for your time, Ser."

Murrough moved around him quickly, and Bray asked one last question. "Where is Daria now?"

Without looking back, he answered, "No one in this town really cares." Then he was gone, heading towards the young woman tending her garden.

~ ~ ~

"I'm not really getting a very cozy vibe here," Varthstone commented with a dour expression on the evening of their second day.

They sat around a small table in an inn called the Penitent Wheel. It was a well-made structure, complete with a full tavern, twin fireplaces, and huge, lavishly decorated rooms full of fineries that Bray would never have a need for. It was the type of lodging reserved for wealthy merchants, or visiting dignitaries. It wasn't Bray's first choice, but he didn't want to stay in an obvious location and project his comings and goings so openly to Adjutant Murrough.

Bray chose not to answer Varthstone's statement, but instead stared at his pint of amber ale in front of him. There was nothing to say. He felt that things seemed off as well. They had questioned various townsfolk for two days on the events that led up to the murder of Gallach, and then Esme's execution. To all of them it seemed matter-of-fact. Esme sinned heavily and she paid the price. The fact that she was set ablaze before Gallach's body even had a chance to cool didn't seem to concern them one bit.

Furthermore, no one wanted to help in locating Daria. Like Adjutant Murrough had proclaimed, no one cared. When she turned her back on the Maker, she turned her back on them.

Her actions angered Aodhfin as well. He believed strongly in his god, he believed in the good of the Enclave. For her to turn away from that, after her father had given so much…

"Why are we 'ere?"

Bray looked up, his anger at Daria momentarily interrupted.

"Why are we 'ere?" Sange quipped again, taking a particularly long draw from her pint. She wiped the froth off her lips with the back of a gloved hand. "The Bishop dinna contact us like the Enclave said, and the case has been solved, haddin' it? I mean, horrific-ally, brutally, savagely solved, but solved," she added, her discontent for the way the wife had been treated seeping through each word.

"Aye," the sorcerer agreed. "Good point. Though, it's 'horrifically', and 'brutally'. You'll learn how to speak like the big boys one day."

Varthstone ignored her withering glare, facing Bray. "What are we still doing here, Purist? I mean ships still in port an' all, we can hop a ride back to the Citadel, report what you found, and none's the wiser."

Sange nodded her agreement, though her look didn't change.

"Just like that?" Bray asked. "A man was murdered, a daughter is missing, and the wife, executed for the crime. All of this doesn't strike you as a little odd?"

"Sure it does," the Elf agreed. "But we're not here for that, we're here for a murder. That's solved. Wife did it." The way he said 'Wife did it' made Bray pause. It didn't sound like he meant it.

"You think she was innocent?" Aodhfin asked.

Varthstone gave a little shrug. "It's not my place to question my employers, but since you're asking, no I don't think she did it. It's like you said, it's a little odd, and a bit too convenient if you ask me."

"I dunna like how everyone jus' accepts it," Sange added. "I mean, Gallach had been here fer a long time right? Did they all hate him or sumtin'?"

"He was an adjutant, and before that, a purist," Bray stated.

"So he was a dick," Sange said.

Bray glowered at her, but it quickly faded when he saw the large smile on her face.

"Yer so serious all the time!" she said jovially, before adding, "I jus' think it's a mite bit odd is all, how they're jus' going about it like nuthin' happened."

"It's almost been a month," Bray interjected.

"Yeah, imagine if someone close to ye died less than a month ago, how would ye feel?" she asked.

Bray winced. He realized how he did feel and Sange was right: they *were* too callous. Why?

"There's also still the matter of the haunting," Lotul's almost songlike voice explained. "We were sent here to tend to that, too."

Bray didn't answer. He stared at the white head bobbing gently atop the crisp golden liquor. Barodin's death hurt him, and they had only been friends for a few winters. Simonis and Murrough had to have known Gallach for decades. Worse, Simonis didn't want them here, and Murrough seemed to not care less. It may be their way of dealing with the grief, but Bray didn't think so. That meant there was someone out there who did care. Someone who left that had the authority to request the dispatch of a purist to properly solve the case.

The exactors continued.

"Who cares 'bout tha place? Suren' the Enclave here doesn't. An' if the daughter's been estranged then she has no rights to it," Sange said matter-of-factly. "Right?"

Varthstone shrugged. "Not my area of expertise. I don't know what would be needed to claim rights."

Then Bray understood. He understood what was happening and why someone had reached out to the Citadel. "They're cutting her out."

Both exactors looked at him. "They don't want a heretic to assume the property. Property owned by a devout man of the cloth. It's a slap in their collective faces." A dawning of comprehension engulfed him. "A will. They need a will."

"Who does?" Sange asked.

"Anyone. Everyone," Bray replied, his energy levels rising. "Gallach's last will and testament will direct who all the assets belong to after he died. Likely it was his wife, but if he put a secondary recipient or even a tertiary…"

"And if there is no will?" Varthstone inquired.

"Then the property and all its fortunes turn over to the Enclave."

Varthstone nodded, "Which in this case is Simonis."

"Even though Daria is still a living heir?" Sange asked, disbelievingly.

Bray nodded, "It is irrelevant. All purists, adjutants too, are required to have a will once they wed. If they don't then all their worldly possessions are subject to the Enclave."

"What kind of timeline are we looking at for that?" Varthstone asked. "Months? Winters?"

"Twenty-five days," Bray replied.

Sange spit her drink out in surprise. "What?"

Aodhfin nodded. It made sense, why they didn't want him here, why they didn't want the exactors around. Everything was falling in place right where they needed it. Everything was just so convenient.

A husband killed by his wife. A conviction and execution immediately follows. A daughter branded a heretic and separated from the church. Brand the home haunted so no one would search it for the will, and you have no clear recipient to the estate. They only needed to hold it like that for twenty-five days, and the Citadel would legally honor all dividends sent to Simonis and the clergy.

Bray didn't want to believe it. He didn't want to think that this was what Simonis may be plotting. A man of the church, a man devoted to the Maker. Nevertheless, something was clearly afoot. There was a reason they were not wanted here. He hoped to the Maker that he was wrong, and it was all a big mistake. Yet he couldn't deny the coincidence, or the fact that no one really seemed that upset over the loss of Gallach and his wife. Bray was short on leads and this seemed like as good as any.

"We have less than forty-eight hours," Bray said.

"Fer what?" Sange asked.

Bray looked at her and felt a certainty in what he need do. "To find the will and find out who really stood to gain by the deaths of Vey Gallach and his wife."

MANOR

"Where do we even begin ta look?" Sange asked, shaking her head.

"Logic says Daria," Bray answered. "She stands to gain the most if the will surfaces."

"No one'll tell us where ta find Daria, and I canna track a ghost in a town full of people," Sange replied.

"Then let's track the ghosts themselves," Varthstone said.

Bray looked at the High Elf. Lotul shrugged, "It's why I'm here, right? I mean aside from my good looks."

Sange rolled her eyes.

"No, he's right," Bray said, looking at the two of them, a plan percolating in his head. "Adjutant Daz picked a sorcerer to deal with a possible haunted manor. I'm no expert on haunting and personally I don't believe in them, but if they do exist then...."

"A miffed spirit migh' tell us where the will is?" Sange asked, not believing her own words.

Varthstone chuckled. "They are more likely to kill you through possession of your muscles, forcing every part of your body into a series of crippling seizures, until it grips your lungs, ruptures blood vessels, and fills them, causing you to drown in your own blood. If you're lucky though, they'll clot your blood instead, and it rushes to your brain. Pop! No more Sange. Or, in the state of your convulsions, you might break your own neck. That would be best I think," he remarked nonchalantly.

Sange fixed Varthstone with a murderous stare.

"I was going to say we should be wary," Bray told them both, ending any debate before Sange pummeled the skinny Elf. "Personally I think it's a trick to keep everyone out of the manor. Once it transfers over to Simonis, I'm sure the ghosts will suddenly just vanish."

"And iffin' it's not?" Sange asked.

"Then I do what I'm paid for," Varthstone said with a smile.

~ ~ ~

An hour later, the trio stood before the large portcullis to Gallach Manor. It was almost pitch black out. A heavy cloud cover drowned out the few stars that dotted the sky, and it happened to be the first night of a new moon.

A blackened iron fence stood eight feet high and ran completely around the perimeter of the property. Before them, the gate hung open only a few inches. It swayed ominously on creaky hinges even though there was no wind. There was a large G gilded onto both sides of the gate in gold. It seemed dull and muted in the dim night.

Bray stared at the gilding, the corners of his eyes etched with concern.

"Second thoughts?" Sange asked as she stared morosely into the void-like courtyard beyond.

He shook his head no. "I'm just wondering how an adjutant, who is supposed to turn away from all worldly possessions, could live in a large manor, with a golden engraved gate?"

"Well, he was retired," Varthstone reminded Bray. "Could that make a difference?"

"I suppose," he agreed.

"Perhaps it's plain in der. Like a monastery." Sange queried. "Or maybe this was one of the only structures they could give 'im at the time."

Bray shot her a patronizing look. She merely shrugged in mock innocence. Slowly he opened the gate and stepped into the courtyard beyond.

Due to the gloominess outside, the manor loomed in front of them like an opaque silhouette. In front of the dusky structure, Aodhfin heard the sounds of trickling water but couldn't quite make out the source.

Their feet crunched against loose pebbles on the cobbled path. Aodhfin noted that everything else was silent. No calls from insects, or hoots from owls, or cries from an errant fox. There was nothing, only the sounds from his feet, the water in front of him, and the heavy breathing behind.

"Well this is cheery," Varthstone said sardonically from behind. "Perhaps we should reconvene when we can see, like the daytime?"

Aodhfin ignored him as they moved forward. They had less than two days to solve a murder or find the will. The obvious choice is that Simonis must have it stowed away trying to hide it until the twenty-five days passed, but Aodhfin didn't think so. If they had it, they wouldn't be going through the ruse that Gallach Manor was haunted. If Daria had it, she would have come forward by now, unless she was dead, and if it was in someone else's possession they were keeping very quiet about it. That left the manor. If any clues were going to point them in the right direction, it would start here.

Abruptly the fountain came into view. It was flat and simple in design. A single round wall rose from the ground, constructed of white marble, and had no ornamentation of any kind. In the center of the pool of water was a raised platform of about four feet. From the top water trickled over, creating curtains of raining crystal clear liquid in a circular pattern down the pedestal and into the pool below.

Ivy had begun to grow over the walls of the fountain, and reached into the edges of the water, like extended fingers stretching for nourishment.

Bray walked up and looked into the pool of water. It was still clear, even in the black of night. Nothing had begun to obscure the waters yet. Again, something didn't sit right. Twenty-three days since Gallach died, the house was vacant, and yet someone was still cleaning algae from a fountain?

He continued through the courtyard until the obscure home came into view. Bray had not ventured so far north in Sentinel's Barrow during the day so he hadn't really gotten to see the estates. Seeing it now though, much like the gate, filled him with anger.

It was a mansion. Distinctive features of the white plaster façade included a massive entablature, and cornices lined with dentils. A row of square, giant order columns on granite bases supported the front. Twelve in all, these columns formed a double gallery. The front staircase had twin sets of stairs on both sides leading upwards toward the open gallery.

No adjutant should live so lavishly.

They carefully climbed the stairs to the gallery above. Bray could see several tall, floor-to-ceiling windows across the gallery's level. They inspected every one, finding them all locked, and heavy crème draperies pulled tightly shut. With no light source evident, the inside of the manor seemed as murky inside as the opaque night that surrounded them.

The trio advanced to the wide cherry wood door. A large custom black iron knocker was installed on the door, and Bray was relieved to see that it, at least, represented the Jasian Enclave.

The knocker was the symbol of Jasia herself. A statuette carved as a beautiful human woman, but bearing features similar to every devoted race. Her height and physical stature were just neutral enough that she could resemble a taller lithe Dwarf, or a slightly buxom Elven woman. To accent this she wore only a simple full-length garment, cinched at the waist. Jasia's hands were clasped together in reverence, for her father above.

She was the mortal daughter of the Maker, the one he had chosen to show the world that Creation is the will of one god, the Maker, not the many. In the end, she was a martyr, sacrificing herself for her beliefs. That sacrifice solidified the true birth of her religion, ultimately turning her fledgling belief into one of the most influential empires on all of Kuldarr.

Seeing that symbol filled him with a glimmer of hope that perhaps not all had been lost with Gallach. Perhaps the adjutant held dear to his principles more than the ostentatious house dictated. Bray wouldn't know of course until he entered the house. He reached out, grabbed the door handle, and pulled.

It didn't budge.

He tried to push on the door, and received the same result.

"Perhaps we should knock?" Varthstone quipped. "How do you use this thing anyway?" The sorcerer went up to the knocker and grabbed the small iron bosoms of the device.

Eyes wide, Bray slapped Varthstone's hands away. Sange snickered behind him. "How dare you desecrate Jasia in such a manner!" the purist seethed.

"You need to calm down, Commander," the Elf retorted, his lips dripping with a mocking woe. "I merely was trying to find that special spot that would open her up."

Sange's snicker turned into a full blurt of laughter. Bray looked incredulously at the two of them. "We are here to try and solve a murder, in the middle of the night, on the doorstep to a manor that might be haunted, and you make jokes? About my faith nonetheless! Are you really as stupid as you look, or is this all just an act to try and see how far you can push me?"

The sorcerer's jeering face fell flat at his eyes condescendingly glared at the purist. "It would not be wise to call a master of **Creation** stupid, priest."

Bray's hand slid to the handle of the war-hammer at his side. Aodhfin's voice was just as icy. "And I would be wary, were I you, of how you choose to act about my religion."

They stared at each other for several moments. Bray could feel the tension rising between the two of them, like a malevolent heat on a midsummer's day. The purist's fingers wrapped around the rough leather banding of the war-hammer's handle. A single phrase, a strange word uttered, and Bray would strike before the sorcerer could finish. They were too close to one another. The Elf would never be able to finish his spell.

Bray could see the same realization being calculated in Varthstone's eyes. The sorcerer knew he couldn't win. Not here.

Instead, he smiled. "Well, I'm glad we've gotten that out of the way then." Slowly he raised his hand to the door. "After you then, purist. Let's see if your god can open the way."

Aodhfin just released his grip from the hammer when, without warning, Sange's large muscular leg lanced forth. Her foot slammed into the door with bone-jarring force, causing whatever was barring the way to splinter and shatter. The door swung inward violently.

"Ye men take too long," she huffed as she stepped inside.

Bray shook his head in frustration. He hated exactors. They had no tact, and no control. Hells, they were damn near untrainable. He wished his unit were here with him, instead of this pathetic lot. They knew how to respond to the situation. His old leader could have handled Varthstone and Sange, he told himself bitterly. Angry beyond words, with more than just the exactors, he followed the mountain of a woman inside.

~ ~ ~

With no light outside and nothing forthcoming from the vacant building, the foyer was so incredibly black that if possible, Bray actually thought it looked blue.

"And we're back to being blind again," Varthstone remarked dryly.

As if his words conjured some mystical spell, suddenly the door slammed shut behind them, sealing them within the absolute darkness.

"What did ye do?" Sange hissed.

"Nothing!" Varthstone spat, a tinge of fear in his voice. "I did nothing!"

Bray wrapped his fingers around his war-hammer and carefully lifted it off the hook at his belt. He felt the weight of it in his hands. He felt more secure when he held his weapon. More alert. He calmly asked, "Did anyone glimpse anything at all before the door closed?"

"No," the hulking warrior woman replied.

"You're joking, right?" The sorcerer replied, "It was too dark *before* the door shut!"

Bray could tell from the timbre of his voice and his erratic breathing that the Elf was close to losing it. Bray had experience in morale failure. He had felt it the first time he was in combat. He had seen it with new recruits. A panicked soldier could break down a whole formation. It was the weakest link of every chain, and often the first thing to fail. When one went, a cascade of fear and failure followed. He didn't need Sange to lose her composure as well. Bray willed himself to remain passive and neutral as he told the

Elf to calm down, that everything would be alright. He didn't allow a tremor to sneak into his voice; he didn't let his own turmoil affect his words. Barodin had always shown him strength, when Bray had flagged. The purist had to do the same now.

"Okay," he heard the sorcerer say, his voice already evening out.

He knew the tranquility of his voice had given the Elf a measure of courage. Now he needed to hold on to it. "Can you find the door?"

"Yes," Varthstone replied.

"Does it open?"

Bray heard it rattle and shake violently. He knew the answer before the Elf even replied, no. "Then we find another way. There are tall windows all around us, we are not trapped in here, we can leave at any time," he said simply. "For now let's set out to complete what we planned on doing."

"We've no light," Varthstone said.

"On it," Sange replied deftly.

Bray heard a clamoring behind him, followed by a loud rip of fabric. Moments later, there was a crash with a litany of curses.

"Sange?"

Without warning fire erupted to life only a few feet in front of him. "Sorry!" Sange apologized. "I dinna know we 'ere so close!"

She moved the open flame from his face and he could see immediately what she had done. Sange had found her way to one of the windows Aodhfin had mentioned, and ripped down the drapes and dowel that had held them in place. She tore long runners from the drapes and wrapped them around the dowel, and had somehow found a way to ignite the material.

"I keep a snifter of oil on me at all times," Sange said, reading the question in his eyes. "And flint."

"Clever girl," Bray returned. Now armed with light, they had a better look at their surroundings.

The foyer was large and circular shaped. The inside walls were lined with rounded ornate columns. Between each column on the south end were the tall windows. As Bray's eyes continued around the room he watched it transition from windows to doors, and finally at the northernmost point were another set of twin stairs. Beneath those stairs was a fireplace and mantle.

The ceiling sat an easy fifteen feet above them, affording him the ability to see a portico on the next floor that led to rooms beyond. Stone-encrusted balustrades protected the portico above.

Bray focused on the fireplace. It was massive, and the mantle and trim around it appeared to be made of marble. Like the balusters above, it held the same stone encrustations.

Bray's and Sange's attention became riveted to what was above the mantle. There on the wall was a full-scale portrait of Esme. What surprised him though, was not the fact that there was a portrait, but how amazingly beautiful the woman was.

A low whistle sounded behind him, conveying his more impure thoughts. Thoughts he quickly pushed from his mind.

"Now that's a looker," Varthstone said.

Bray even saw Sange nodding in agreement.

"And they put her to torch?" the Elf continued. "Such a waste."

Strangely enough, Aodhfin agreed with the sorcerer. Her beauty was a rare kind. Exotic, with black hair that was long and full. It flowed luxuriously down to the small of her back. Vibrant emerald green orbs that were almond shaped glittered at them. High cheekbones, a thin nose, and full lips rounded out all the high points of her looks, but it was her jawline that he found, strangely, the most alluring. She had a strong jaw, almost like a man's. It was full with a square chin. Normally, Bray would have found such a thing almost too masculine, marring natural feminine beauty. On her though, it seemed… perfect. It gave her a presence that was hard to ignore. Just the sight of her was mesmerizing, and it was merely a painting.

Underneath her were the name Esme Gallach, and a date. The painting was only two winters old.

"How old was Gallach?" Sange asked, looking with concern at the picture.

Bray shrugged. He didn't know.

"This girl looks like she's in er' mid-twenties," Sange remarked. "I was a guessin' Daria was grown, by the way people spoke."

"As did I," Bray agreed. "Even if she married when she was sixteen, as is Enclave tradition, the daughter couldn't be more than what… ten, maybe eleven?"

"We need ta find that will," Sange said a little desperately. "No child deserves ta be made poor afta losin' their parents."

Again, Bray found himself in agreement with the exactor. It was wrong what they were doing to this child, regardless of belief, but was it true?

Bray still couldn't think that the Bishop was capable of such a dark act, yet with nothing else to go on he found he couldn't refute it, either. Simonis was involved with the murder in some capacity. It was up to Bray to find out just how involved.

HAUNT

They moved through the house for the better part of the next hour. Sange created two more torches for Bray and Varthstone out of the rest of the drapes and the legs off a chair from the dining room. As Bray held the sturdy polished oak in his left hand, he didn't even want to think how expensive the chair might have been.

They had tried to light the sconces on the walls, as well as the fireplace itself, but there was no good wood remaining, nor was there enough oil. So they traveled through the dark house as if it was some sort of dungeon and they intrepid adventurers.

Now Bray didn't think highly of exactors-- he thought they were all jackboots and thugs--and up until now, that impression had held. Yet he was surprised to see the two with him now move with purpose. As they inspected room after room on the first floor, they passed up countless valuables, from fine china, to jewelry, to expensive baubles that seemed to have no purpose, all likely to fetch a decent sum of money to the perceptive entrepreneur. Yet even the sharp-tongued sorcerer seemed determined to do his job. As much as he didn't like to admit it to himself, their dedication impressed him.

After checking every room on the first floor and the cellar, they found nothing that could even give a remote hinting towards a will or marital problems. There were portraits of the two of them, the adjutant and his wife, throughout the manor, and they looked happy. Bray supposed such things could be deceiving, with a dark reality bubbling underneath the surface of the beautifully painted works of art.

Outside of the door slamming and locking them in, they had not encountered any poltergeists of any kind. Bray had almost convinced himself that it must have been the wind. Almost. It was on the second floor that things began to change.

Bray led the formation as they moved up the gently winding stairs to the second floor. Halfway up he caught a movement by the balusters out of the corner of his eye. He wheeled the torch in the direction of the movement, red-orange light sputtering.

Sange drew her axe at his sudden turn. "What?" she whispered.

Bray shook his head. There was nothing there. Nothing at all.

"It's… nothing," he finally relented. "Let's go."

The purist stepped onto the portico, gingerly, as a feeling of worry began to grow in his gut. Something was different on this floor. He looked to his exactors. If they felt it too, they did not show it.

Lavish furniture dotted the backs of the walls, and Bray was forced to make a choice between the door on the left, and on the right. On the other floors, that hadn't mattered to him, they just split up to cover more ground. Now the twisting he felt in his innards only brought apprehension.

He decided left.

As the three of them walked through the doorway, all hell broke loose.

~ ~ ~

A blood-curdling scream sliced through the air and cut into the trio like daggers in their flesh. It was earsplitting and guttural. Bray immediately raised his hammer, ready for whatever was about to attack.

Varthstone spun around frantically. "Behind us... the stairs!" he yelled, raising a hand in defense.

"Over there!" Sange screamed, pointing at the opposite door on the portico just as it slammed shut.

Bray too saw something in front of him, a shimmering form in his flickering amber glow. It looked like a woman in a soft chemise. It hugged her sultry form as she moved forward towards him. Bray closed his eyes. *I do not believe in ghosts*, he told himself. *I do not believe in ghosts.* He opened his eyes.

She was still there.

She looked at him sorrowfully, her emerald green eyes pouring themselves over him like a pitcher of ice-cold water. He felt himself shaking. "No," he growled. Bray stepped forward.

Suddenly the wraith screamed a banshee's wail once more. Her body erupted into flames and she ran down the hallway.

Bray turned to see if it had been the work of the sorcerer, but he saw immediately that it was not the case. Lotul was busy fighting his own phantoms. Flickering shards of ice flew out towards the balustrades from his extended fingertips. Lotul's torch lay on its side on the ground. The flame guttered. What the Elf was fighting, Bray couldn't see.

Sange was across the portico slamming her axe into the heavy door over and over again, like a lumberjack chopping down a tree. She seemed enraged, screaming so hard her vocal cords were tearing. Wood splintered with every massive impact from her muscle-laden arms. She would be through the door in no time, the purist reasoned.

Then Bray felt cold. Something like ice water rushed down his spine. He froze in place, and yet something turned him, controlled him.

He faced back down the hallway and she was there again, the spirit. Bray recognized her. She was the same lovely creature that he saw in the portrait downstairs. Esme.

She beckoned him forward with a thin ivory finger. Woodenly, his muscles reacted, convulsing in pain as he fought it. First he made one step, then another.

Esme took a step backwards, her eyes like viridian fire never leaving his face. They went down the hallway together, and Bray had no choice but to leave his companions behind, fighting their own battles.

He turned down another hall, and then turned again. Before he knew it, he was facing towards the courtyard once more. A towering picture window showed him the night beyond.

Esme reached out and touched the window. Frost ran across the pane of glass from her fingertip. It spread throughout the window like a spider's web. A weave of glittering crystals danced along its surface, reflecting like a thousand diamonds against the amber light of his torch.

Then the window was full, the bitter frost encased the whole sheet of glass like a veil. Bray heard the high-pitched whine of the thin windowpane followed by a snap.

Where Esme touched the pane was a small crack. There was a sheering sound and within a fraction of a second Bray watched, helpless, as the long lines arced and crisscrossed against the frost-laden panel.

It exploded. Shards of sharpened icy glass flew outward like glimmering daggers into the darkness of night. Immediately, warm, salty air slapped his face. In the distance, he could hear the thunderous roll of waves as they crashed ashore.

Bray felt his legs moving once more. One step. Another. He struggled against the feeling, his legs cramping and trembling. He wanted to scream in pain, but he couldn't fight it. She was too strong. He stepped up against the frame. He dropped his hammer to the ground and reached out to steady himself. His bare hand leaned against the sharp, cold glass. It bit into his flesh. Bray ignored the burn of the piercing shard that coursed through his hand. His sole concern was on the ground that loomed up at him from twenty feet below.

Hard cobblestones glared up at him expectantly. Aodhfin knew he had to win this fight, but she was so strong. Then his eyes fell to the fountain beneath him. He could now see that the flat simple design from below was actually a circumpunct, the symbol of the Jasian Enclave.

The purist prayed to the Maker for strength. He fought against the spirit with all he had. His muscles rippled in strain underneath his armor. His body quaked as he tried to deny her his body. His right foot lifted, and he felt himself lean forward. His whole body pitched forward, and the ground below was all he saw as the wind blew against his face. His torch toppled forward, cartwheeling out below him until it struck the ground in a flash of sparks. And then he was falling out after it.

THE SCENE

Thick arms like tree trunks wrapped around him just as his feet broke the plane of the windowsill. "Bray!" the voice bellowed in alarm. "Bray!"

His feet slammed back down against the frame, but his doeskin boots shuffled and slid forward. Aodhfin's mind was a haze. He couldn't muster any thoughts except that he was falling. Esme threw him from the window! He was falling!

"Pull him back," another voice said through the murk. There was a songlike eloquence to it. "Stupid, idiot purist."

Aodhfin watched in alarm as the ground pulled away from him. Slowly he was drug backwards until he saw a cherry wood frame shrouded with fragments of broken glass. One of them was covered in blood.

There was a loud groan as the big arms wrapped around his chest tighter and fiercely yanked him up and over. Then he was falling again, this time backwards as he toppled onto the person who had stopped him from jumping.

His head slammed against the wall as they fell, jarring him and causing the room to spin. A ringing sound echoed in his ears.

Aodhfin fell against something soft. It was supple and velvety against the side of his face.

"Do ye mind?" a distinctly feminine voice asked.

Aodhfin blinked several times trying to shake away the disorientation. He raised his head slowly, and was alarmed to see Sange's doe brown eyes looking down her nose at him only a few inches away.

It was then that Aodhfin realized where he landed. Sange's bosom. Or what she had of one anyhow. He pulled up quickly, embarrassed. "Sorry," he muttered.

Sange smiled.

The sorcerer behind them snickered. "You can get a room together later," he remarked snidely. "In the meantime, gather your wits purist. We're here."

Bray shook the cobwebs from his head. "Here?" he questioned. "But Esme! Watch for her spirit!"

He was surprised to see Lotul shaking his head. "I'll explain later, priest. Right now we have a crime scene to case." The sorcerer pointed to the room next to them.

Aodhfin followed the Elf's finger through the doorway, and he saw it clearly. The master bedroom. The place where Esme had killed Gallach.

The purist stood and extended his hand to help the large woman up. They both saw it running red with blood. "Bray!" Sange said in alarm.

Aodhfin pulled his hand back as the bitter sting suddenly began to throb throughout is hand. "It's nothing," he remarked. Aodhfin looked into a satchel on his belt and quickly removed gauze to wrap it. He kept it for such a purpose. When done, he hefted up his hammer and put it back on the hook at his waist.

He followed Varthstone into the room.

"Don't touch anything," he reminded them, though it seemed that the sorcerer needed no such prodding. It was apparent that he knew his way around a crime scene.

The room was large, at least half the size of the foyer. The floors were all a cherry wood, and the walls a crème stucco plaster. It was very different from the other rooms they had encountered. Cozy.

Against the east wall were two large windows. Not the full-size windows he had seen in the foyer, but smaller, only running from two feet off the ground to about eight feet high. White sheer curtains hung wistfully between crimson silk drapes. Out those windows, he could see the winking lights of lanterns half a mile away. Adjutant Murrough's estate.

Bray directed his gaze to the perimeter of the room. Chaise lounges dotted the four corners, each with ornate engraved end tables between them. A 'G' was hand embroidered into each one. Every chair seemed to be made of suede, and colored the same crème color as the walls.

A large fireplace adorned the southern wall.

In the center of the room was the bed. A massive four-poster that held a thick feather mattress and a dozen goose down pillows, all of them covered in silk sheeting the same crimson as the drapes. There were no dressers, chests, or armoires for clothing, nor were there closets of any kind. There was an attached room directly next to them, but Bray could see it led to a bathing area.

This wasn't a standard bedroom for a retired adjutant looking to slumber within. This room was a shrine.

Aodhfin could only stare. This was not how an adjutant was supposed to live his life in service of the Maker.

The purist's eyes drifted to where the altercation had taken place, directly next to the bed. Dried blood, now brown and flaky, had sprayed violently against the walls. There was a similar jet of crusted blood against the left foot poster of the bed. This had apparently run rich, as the sheets in that corner were soaked liberally. The overturned chair was adorned with bloodied handprints. On the floor an oblong, brown stain was now soaked into the pores of the wood. At the center of that stain sat a long-bladed dagger, jewel-encrusted, and covered up to the hilt in the dried morass.

Small feminine fingerprints could be seen across the room, on the dagger, the chaise, the bed, and even an end table. All, presumably, from the victim's blood.

Sange said what they all were thinking. "Tis a lot of blood."

"Too much," Varthstone replied as he walked around the throne-like bed.

Without touching anything, he pointed to the walls. "You see the spray pattern here," he explained. "She hit a major artery. Otherwise, there should be no reason for such a projection. Look how high and far it reaches, look at the arc pattern," he pointed out. "She knew exactly what she was doing, in which case this is now premeditated. A crime of passion is sudden. A burst of unexpected violence. Anger and frustration are equal tools just as any dagger may be. There are repeated stabbings. This causes the blood to gush, or pour, not spray. Normally, the aggressor would get doused more liberally, and anything within direct proximity, say the bed. To me this room appears staged."

Aodhfin looked at the Varthstone in surprise. "Staged?"

The Elf nodded. "In the High Province, we call this an orgy of evidence. Look at the clues laid out for us to see, still untouched, due to the 'convenience' of the haunting."

"But it is haunted."

Again, Varthstone shook his head. "I'll explain later. In the meantime we focus on this murder."

Bray nodded. The exactor was right. He needed to focus on what was in front of him.

"Why is dis' 'ere an orgy?" Sange asked.

Varthstone smiled in his condescending way. "I'm glad someone is paying attention." He pointed to the dagger on the floor. "So our murderer thrusts this weapon into her husband, for argument's sake severs an artery, and then what? In a true crime of passion, she would keep stabbing, randomizing the pattern of arterial spray. Or freak out and either try to stem the bleeding, or flee. We know she didn't run, so why didn't she use the bedding to soak up the blood? Look at the patterns of the blood, precision strikes. Look where her 'handprints' are all located. What was she doing? Crawling?"

He pointed to the floor where the stain was greatest. "Let's just say it was a kill shot. She goes numb at what she did, so she just drops the dagger next to the body? Then she remains standing until she is apprehended, barefoot, at that."

"How?" Sange began, but Bray quickly answered. "Look at the stains on the floor, just out of the puddle," he said. "There are slight impressions, seven per step. Five for toes, one for the pad, the other for the heel. She has arched feet. A boot or slipper would be a single impression."

"Precisely," Varthstone replied. "Yet look at the rest of the floor. No other tracks, no foot prints at all, yet we have a bevy of handprints everywhere. Handprints being the easiest to compare to the alleged killer. Yet how could those handprints, which are more than likely Esme's, have gotten there, without her moving. Furthermore, how did they get her out, if she wasn't walking? What we have here is a "razzle-dazzle", people."

Aodhfin looked at the Elf with a raised eyebrow.

Varthstone lowered his eyes to the floor and shook his head. "How did they ever put you in charge?" he asked, before answering Aodhfin's silent query. "Overload the senses with the blatantly obvious," he said, pointing to the handprints, the knife, and the copious amounts of blood. "Your mind immediately assigns guilt. Esme at the scene, handprints match hers. Factor in a loud argument, and you have a crime of passion. Add to it a haunting and you reduce any suspicion by eliminating a follow-up after the initial inspection. Razzle the senses. Dazzle the mind," he said in finality, folding his arms.

"So…," Sange began.

"He's saying that Esme's been framed," Aodhfin said in understanding. "And the real killer is still out there."

THE GLYPH

Aodhfin took the news in stride. The killer is still at large, he echoed to himself. They executed the wrong person! Esme was innocent. No wonder she was haunting the manor.

Flexing his lacerated hand, he walked over to the fireplace to think. He was careful not to touch anything at the scene, or risk contaminating it worse than it already was.

He watched as Varthstone hiked up his robes so he could get closer to the floor to analyze how Gallach might have fallen, which position he might have lain that would explain why so much blood had gotten everywhere.

Sange fell back towards the entrance, and Aodhfin could tell she looked pale. While the large woman may not run from any battle, the sight of such a brutal murder unsettled her.

As Aodhfin turned once more to evaluate the scene, a strange glimmer caught his eye. He followed it. It was the mantle above the fireplace, or more accurately a vase.

The purist leaned forward and examined the porcelain container. It was lavender in color and looked to have held a bouquet of flowers. The lilies that had been within were now all curled and dead. There was something unusual about them though. The desiccated petals had markings on them.

"Varthstone," Bray called, still studying the strange symbols.

He felt the presence of Lotul as the sorcerer came up beside him, a curtain of blonde hair separated his face from Bray's. "What is it?"

Aodhfin pointed.

He watched as the Elf leaned forward, studying the vase, and then his eyes went wide in shock. He looked over to Bray. "Do you know what this is?" he said with a smile.

Bray shook his head no. That was why he had a sorcerer there, after all. "These are glyphs," he said in a burble. "The ones on the petals are sound-based, they pick up ambient noise. The shimmering one on the vase though, it's ocular."

"What does that mean?" the purist asked with a shrug.

The Elf's clean face was almost jubilant. "It means that someone out there witnessed the murder. It means that someone in this town is a sorcerer. And that, Ser, is someone I can find."

~ ~ ~

They knew they had to wait until the next day before they could move again. So, the trio retreated to the inn where Aodhfin had cleaned and stitched his wound, and caught a few hours rest. When he had awoken, he felt refreshed in body, but not in mind. Aodhfin was troubled. He was troubled at the possible implications of what they'd discovered inside the manor. Men of faith were committing terrible sins within Sentinel's Barrow. Men that he had respected. A bishop, an adjutant...

Aodhfin may have been naïve to the touch of a woman, but he knew what he had seen in that bedroom. It had been designed for one purpose, and one purpose alone. Sex.

It went against all that Aodhfin had believed purists to be: men of sanctity, men of the Maker. Yes, he understood the necessity of procreation, and that it was an enjoyable act. Nevertheless, the bed had all but been a shrine. Sex had become an instrument of Gallach's faith, and that should not be.

When he met later with the exactors, he shook himself of the demons of doubt that plagued him. He needed to find out what was happening in this town. He needed to find the errant killer. The smug smile on the sorcerer's face told Bray that the next step was going to be easy.

"I've got him," Varthstone said as Bray approached.

"You've been out already this morning?" Aodhfin asked.

The Elf shook his head no. Instead, he held up one of the dead lilies he had taken from the vase. "I counter-scryed the glyph. He tried to use it this morning, and I've got him."

Bray had no idea what the sorcerer was talking about, but if it led them to the witness, then that was good enough for him. "Who is it?"

Sange spoke up. "I **have** been out fer the sorcerer doin' a wee bit o' scoutin'. Turns out, there issin' Al-key-mist."

"Alchemist" Varthstone corrected.

"What I said," Sange countered, before continuing. "Alchemist in town that's good wit' flowers. An Elf whose name we already know."

"Fem Fonzil?" Bray asked.

The Elf nodded. "Turns out our mortician multitasks, and dabbles in a little sorcery too."

"He also has help. We saw 'er from afar day we arrived. When ye was speakin' wit Murrough," Sange added.

Bray nodded. "I remember. Black hair. She was tending a garden."

"And a direct line to Murrough," Sange added. "Perhaps a lion-son?"

"Liaison," Varthstone corrected again.

"Quit it," Sange snapped.

Bray grimaced. He didn't like to implicate the adjutant. "What is his motive though?" the purist asked. "Though I am loath to admit it, the Bishop has more to gain than anyone else from Gallach's death, save their daughter. Murrough though…"

"Don't rule him out because he's one of you," Varthstone said matter-of-factly.

Heat rose to Bray's face. Anger bit into his every word. "We have a chain of command here, exactor. Remember your place."

Sange put a comforting hand on his forearm. "Lotul is only statin' what we're all thinkin'. Dunna take it out on him," she replied to Bray softly.

Aodhfin nodded and stowed his frustration. He knew Sange was right. He had been thinking the very same since the night before. "Let's just go speak with our mortician friend."

An hour later, they were in the foyer of a funeral home. Soft golden wooden walls seemed to encase the trio gently. A smell of incense burned lightly in the air. Fem Fonzil sat before them, his long pale fingers interlaced on top of the table they all shared. Four cups of tea sat between them all, none of them touched.

Like Lotul, Fem Fonzil was a pale Elf with almond shaped blue eyes and dark blonde hair. Unlike the sorcerer though, he kept that hair cut short, so the pointed tips of his ears were clearly visible. The mortician wore dark pantaloons and a pressed grey shirt, whose sleeves were rolled up to his elbows.

Bray thought he was going to have to strong-arm Fem Fonzil into talking. He couldn't have been more wrong.

Tears lined the mortician's blue eyes. "Yes, they were my glyphs," he answered honestly. "I arranged them there about three months ago."

"Why?" Bray asked.

"I had to know who else."

"Whaddya mean?" Sange asked him.

His watery eyes looked at them all. Bray saw a bit of surprise in his eyes. "Bishop... Simonis didn't tell you?"

Aodhfin shook his head no.

Fem Fonzil buried his face in his hands, "Maker help me," the Elf sniffed once and looked back up at them, forcing his tears to stop. "Esme and I were intimate."

The news came as a shock to Bray,and he blinked several times in confusion. Yet when he looked at his exactors, they didn't seem at all surprised. Just how naïve was he?

Fem Fonzil continued, "We began having an affair about eighteen winters ago."

"Wait," Varthstone interrupted. "I'm sorry but I have to ask, how old was Esme?"

"Forty-winters-old," he said wistfully. "She was a timeless beauty. The Maker had truly blessed her, and cursed her."

"Go on," Bray told the mortician.

"When we first met, I knew immediately that Esme was a lustful woman who wasn't receiving the satisfaction a lady like her required. When Gallach left on a crusade, I politely interjected myself into her life," he said with a tight smile. "She did not oppose it."

Fem Fonzil looked forlornly out the window towards the Gallach Manor. "She was not happy with her place with Gallach, but the Jasian Enclave forbids divorce from a member of the clergy. To do so is tantamount to death. Gallach was no fool. He realized his beautiful bride was unhappy, and so he lavished her with treasures the best he could. They did not please him, as it was not his station, but he had hoped to win her heart with material trinkets.

"It didn't work of course. Her heart required more than material love, and her body deserved more than passionless intercourse," Fem Fonzil shook his head. "I did not hate Vey Gallach, but I was jealous that he was able to keep his wife, while I had to be an Elf of the shadows."

"Did ye kill 'im'?" Sange asked.

His blue eyes went wide. "Maker no!"

"What happened to change your position with Esme?" Lotul interrupted Sange's blunt remark. "Why did she cut you off after almost two decades of adultery?"

Fem's eyes darted to the other High Elf. "It was her daughter. She had just turned her back on the Enclave and renounced the Maker. Secretly, Esme was proud of Daria. She did not want her daughter to have to walk in the same footsteps as she, marrying a man she didn't love, and living a life she didn't want. I thought it an opportunity."

He looked back to Bray. "I asked her to leave with me. Return to the High Province. I thought she might take strength, like her daughter had shown."

"She refused you," Aodhfin said.

Fem Fonzil nodded, tears welling back up in his red, swollen eyes. "She said I had become too attached, and she broke it off."

"So being the florist as well, you sent those flowers to see if she became involved with another?" Varthstone asked. Fem Fonzil nodded and Bray could see fury replace the heartbreak.

"Who was it?" Bray asked.

Those now cold eyes looked at him, "The correct question to ask is who wasn't it?"

Bray and Sange stiffened. "What do you mean?" the purist asked.

Fem Fonzil scoffed, "I had been living a lie, thinking I was the only one that had caught her interests. It was why I said she was cursed. Esme had a lusting that was insatiable. She was hungry, always hungry, and I don't mean for food. I had thought myself to be feeding that need well, but I was wrong. She sampled from more than just I."

"Murrough?" Varthstone asked, and Bray winced.

To his surprise, Fem Fonzil nodded. "Simonis, too."

Dismayed, Aodhfin pointed a finger at the mortician and growled. "Don't defile their names with slander and accusations."

Fem Fonzil stared at him in shock.

Sange once more tried to talk him down. "Bray, we knew dis was a possibility. We talked about dis."

Aodhfin shook his head, a hot fury building in his heart. "Not this! I accepted that perhaps Simonis was trying to acquire material wealth, take advantage of a situation where he could push out someone who turned their back on the Maker, but not this. Adultery? Murder?"

Aodhfin lunged over the table and grabbed Fem Fonzil's tunic. "I want proof!"

Sange grabbed his shoulders and pulled him back, as Varthstone stood and moved around the table to separate the purist from the mortician.

Sange got them apart, and Fem Fonzil looked at Bray with a combination of anxiety and outrage. "Fine, purist, you want proof, you shall have it. You can have all of it!"

ONLY HUMAN

They stood before a strange round table about the size of a dining table for a family of four. At the outskirts of the table a series of glyphs, similar to what he saw on the vase, danced and glittered. In the center was a circular piece of reflecting glass. Aodhfin knew that reflecting glass was very expensive, so this bizarre bauble must have cost the mortician a small fortune.

What troubled Aodhfin wasn't the expense of the table, but what was within. It was bizarre looking into the glass and expecting to see your own reflection, but instead looking into another room completely. It was like peeking through a window into someone's house to spy on them, yet Bray wasn't seeing into the room now, but looking at the past.

Bray watched, to his revulsion, as a series of suitors came calling on the beautiful woman Esme, each set upon sating her carnal desires. They left thinking themselves triumphant, yet Aodhfin could see that wasn't the case. There was not enough for the woman before him. She was hungry, ravenous for her desires. It was beyond excess. In some instances, he witnessed her having multiple suitors in a single day, some only minutes apart. She had become an expert at it, hiding it from Gallach, and everyone else in town. As Fem Fonzil had been, each man had thought him her only affair.

Then he saw what revolted him most. The bishop. She took him on, like all the others, and his obese frame answered in kind. The sight made him sick to his stomach. Not because it was an elderly fat man getting off on a beautiful woman, but because this man was the voice of the Maker. His decrees were as if the Maker spoke directly. To watch this... defilement... of everything Aodhfin believed in, brought a bitter taste to his mouth, and rolled his guts in anger and sorrow.

"We're only human," Sange said to Aodhfin as she put her strong hand on his shoulder. Clearly, she could see the disgust and bewilderment written across his face.

"I've seen enough," Bray snapped harshly. "Show me the murder."

Fem Fonzil looked at him, and Bray saw the pain in his eyes for having to watch what his beloved did behind his back time after time. The purist wondered how it felt for the Elf in front of him, each time he watched. Like a wicked wound torn open repeatedly.

Fem Fonzil made some form of incantation with his fingers, and one of the glyphs began to shimmer brighter than the rest. The image was different now. The back of a man entered into view, the circle within a circle emblazoned upon his tabard clear to them, the plume of a feather sticking from his cap. Aodhfin seethed at the man... Murrough.

The adjutant began to disarm himself, first removing a gem-encrusted dagger and setting it down, and then his sword. Aodhfin hadn't noticed on their meeting the amount of frivolities he kept upon him. It should have been a sign! He should have known!

Before the man could take off his tabard there was a loud bang, and an older well-built man entered holding a cudgel.

Though in the twilight winters of his life he still bore a broad chest and keen eyes, Aodhfin recognized him from the portraits: Vey Gallach.

He swung the cudgel, striking Murrough across the back. The man moaned and tumbled, knocking over the chaise. Gallach did not relent, slamming the weapon repeatedly into his shoulders, chest, and back. They could hear him yelling 'betrayer!' and 'sinner!' repeatedly at the man. Finally Murrough relented to the elder, picked up his sword and fled.

Gallach wheeled on his wife, and to Aodhfin's surprise, he began to cry. Esme, however, seemed cold to his emotion, aloof. She stood up, walked over to the elder man, and slapped him hard in the face.

Sange gasped.

Gallach was equally surprised. His tears were replaced with a righteous rage. He grabbed Esme by the shoulders and began shaking her violently, screaming at her for why she had continued to betray him.

A sultry smiled played about her lips, and as he continued to get worked up in fury, she began to undo her chemise. Gallach saw this in alarm, and Aodhfin was baffled as well. She was becoming aroused by his anger. She tried to pull him to the bed, tried to win him over with her natural charms, but Gallach was too far gone. He pulled away from her. They all heard him clearly say. "It's over, Esme."

She shot off the bed and apologized to him profusely, but he was shaking his head. "I cannot live like this anymore," he explained. "I've lost everything trying to help you. I've sacrificed everything. Even our own daughter resents what we have become. I will not lose my sanity over this as well. I'm sorry my love, but I must cast you out."

Esme dropped to her knees at his side, now crying and begging forgiveness. Pleading that there was something wrong with her, that she was broken, and he, like the Maker, should forgive her of her sins. However, Gallach was done; the purist could see it all over his face.

Gallach went to leave, when in desperation, Esme lunged for the dagger that Murrough had left behind. She drew the weapon on Gallach, and he looked upon her with pity. Esme stood and flanked him, moving to block his escape. Her back was to the glyph now, so that all they could see was the corner of her crème white shoulder and the long flowing raven black hair. The image faded for a moment.

"What was that?" Bray asked.

Fem Fonzil shook his head, "It's nothing. It happens now and again. I could show you countless other images that I have in regards to this where it has happened. Sometimes if someone close has magical prowess or a magical trinket themselves, it causes a momentary disruption in the scrying. It will come back, and unfortunately you will not miss a thing."

And indeed the image did reappear, just as Esme lunged at Gallach. The older man's eyes were wide with terror, which Aodhfin had found odd considering this was a man who had seen the horrors of war for decades. His attempts to block the dagger were feeble, and Esme's skill and deftness for striking at major arteries were definitely visible.

She plunged the weapon into his right thigh, and Gallach moaned in agony, but did little to stop her. She twisted the weapon and yanked it free, sidestepping the gout of blood that erupted with it, dousing the bed.

She then slid the dagger just under his armpit, erupting another major artery. Blood plumed, rich and vibrant down his yellow tunic, soaking it instantly.

Gallach dropped to his knees, his life's essence jetting out of him in sporadic pulses. He looked up glassy-eyed at the woman before him. Her back to the glyph, she rose the dagger high, and swiped down in a single fatal stroke.

The jugular severed on the elder's neck, a geyser of hot acrid spray splashed against the wall. He toppled over onto his side, blood hemorrhaging out of all of his wounds at an alarming rate. Esme turned to face the glyph and the image faded again.

They all sat mute, waiting for the image to come back. When it did, Esme was crawling back into the picture. She seemed confused. She crawled right into the blood and hefted herself by her hands up the chaise and onto the bed. When she turned around, Aodhfin watched as clarity set in. Esme screamed and dropped to the body. Her hands found the dagger on the floor, picked it up, and she screamed again.

Suddenly Murrough was there, bursting into the room. He stared at the scene, utterly dumbfounded. He began to yell at Esme to drop the weapon while she sobbed. The adjutant approached her slowly, his hands up in alarm. She turned and saw him, saw she was holding the knife and dropped it.

Esme looked at him, desperate and lost, and then as all the events seemed to come down on her at once, she fainted. Murrough managed to catch her before she hit the ground. He lifted her up and carried her from the scene, his feet never once encountering the blood.

They all sat still as they watched the life ebb away from Gallach, as the blood slowed to little more than a trickle and soak into the cherry wood floors.

~ ~ ~

"That's why he responded so quickly," Varthstone said, breaking the silence. "He was there when the murder took place."

Sange nodded and pointed out, "His dagger, too."

"But he is not an accomplice," Bray defended.

Varthstone raised an eyebrow. Aodhfin could tell he was going to retort, but quickly raised his hand. "This is not the place."

The Elf closed his mouth, stared at the Purist harshly for a moment and then nodded. Aodhfin turned to the mortician. "Were you watching this as it happened?" he demanded.

Fem Fonzil shook his head no. "Often I am not here to watch them at the time they are happening. Each glyph here can hold the information only once. Once it is disenchanted, it is gone."

"But you just showed it to us," Bray said.

Varthstone nodded. "But time is limited with a scrying glyph. It takes a spot on this table, and if one wants to scry again he needs to free a spot, rendering this vision abolished."

Bray understood. "You are not to destroy that vision, am I clear?"

The mortician nodded. "Yes, Purist."

"Does anyone else know about this? About your scrying?"

Fem Fonzil shook his head. "No one. Do you know what the bishop would do to me if they learned I had this! If the bishop learned there was a sorcerer even present in Sentinel's Barrow! Not even my apprentice, Nayria, knows about it."

"You are sure?" Bray asked.

The High Elf nodded. "Absolutely."

While Aodhfin wanted to say that Simonis was a Maker- fearing man, and no harm would come to Fem Fonzil for his indiscreet scrying, the purist wasn't so sure anymore.

"Is there any way to transfer that glyph?" Aodhfin asked.

Fem Fonzil shrugged. "Not that I'm aware of."

Aodhfin was going to press when Varthstone spoke up. "I hear that some of my other kin, Wild Elves in particular, are well-versed at scrying and transferring it. We High Elves, though, have no such means."

Bray sighed. Wild Elves secluded themselves from societies and he didn't know where any of their insular villages might be located within Gurgen. They preferred the large forested regions to the east, and Bray knew they didn't have that kind of time.

"We need to find Daria," he said.

"Or the will," Sange returned.

"Well... I might know where the will is," Fem Fonzil said as he began covering up the scrying table.

Everyone looked at the mortician. "Gallach was a pious man, and he spent most of his time at church praying."

"You think the bishop has it?" Bray asked.

Fem Fonzil shook his head. "Not that church," he returned. "Don't get me wrong, he was a man of the Enclave, have no doubt, but he was a solemn man, deeply introverted. He used the abandoned cathedral, the one for the old gods."

"How do you know all this?" Aodhfin asked as he scrutinized the Elf.

Fem Fonzil sighed as he put his face in his hands. He looked at them, forlorn. "You forget so soon that I was bedding his wife. You think I would not trace the steps of the husband?"

"Good point," Varthstone added.

A door closed behind them just as the mortician finished covering the table. Aodhfin was surprised to see it looked just like an alchemist's workstation now.

"Ah, Nayria!" Fem Fonzil said, suddenly jubilant.

Bray turned to look at the person entering and was momentarily taken aback. The young woman before him was simply exquisite. Long black hair encased her delicate and soft Elf-like features. She looked at them all with surprised green eyes that twinkled like gemstones. They were almond shaped just like an Elf's. She had a thin nose and full lips that demanded attention. He noted a very faint point at the tips of her ears. There was something strikingly familiar about her.

"You're a Manhym, a half-elf," Varthstone remarked before Aodhfin could say anything.

"Yes," she said quietly. Then she directed her gaze to the mortician. "Ser Fonzil, I was unaware we had guests."

Fem smiled a genuine smile. "They were just leaving, dear apprentice." He looked at Bray. "The old church has wards crafted by your priests so that only a single key can gain access to it." He dropped his voice to a whisper. "It is likely it's there that he stored whatever was precious to him that he wanted to keep from anyone else."

Bray nodded. "Where do I find this key?"

Fem Fonzil's eyes glittered in a dark way and Bray knew he wasn't going to like what he heard next. "Gallach still has the key on him."

GRAVEYARD

"At least it's not as dark tonight," Sange remarked, looking at the bevy of stars in the sky.

Bray shook his head. "I can't believe I'm about to do this."

Varthstone smiled. "It is a very impure thing to do, isn't it?" The Elf leaned on his shovel as he looked at the uncomfortable purist.

Aodhfin Bray ignored the jibe and the trio walked quietly into the Enclave's graveyard. The small resting place for the deceased was located on the west end of town, nestled between the Enclave to the east, town housing to the north, and the old cathedral to the south. All to the west was the deep blue of Sowle Sea and the loud crashing of the surf.

The whole area was dank.

"You do realize when we start digging we are going to hit water fast. You know what water has likely done to Gallach's body over the last twenty plus days?" Varthstone continued.

Bray shook his head. "Let's try not to think about it, shall we?"

As they quietly walked into the graveyard, Aodhfin fell back to walk side by side with Varthstone. The Elf eyed him curiously, but Bray needed to know what the sorcerer knew about the manor. It had been troubling him all day. "You said we'd talk later about the haunting."

Lotul nodded, "I did."

After a short silence, Aodhfin shot him a look. The Elf sighed. "Okay. The house wasn't haunted."

"But... I saw Esme. She tried to throw me from a window!" he whispered harshly.

"We all saw something," Varthstone returned. "Each what we feared most at the time. That was the nature of the trap. It was very cunning."

"Trap?"

The Elf nodded. "An illusion trap, triggered to the doors on the second floor. I only figured it out after...," he coughed nervously into his hand, "well, after my rather embarrassing episode of attacking the stairs."

"What was your fear?" Bray asked. "And how did you figure out it was an illusion?"

Varthstone appeared momentarily skittish about revealing his fear, but finally he just chuckled and said, "I really hate clowns."

"Clowns? Like jesters that paint their faces and do stupid things?"

Varthstone sighed and looked to the stars. "Yes," he admitted. "They just... they really bother me."

Aodhfin suppressed a laugh. "I can see that," he agreed.

The Elf continued, "That's how I knew it was an illusion. The sorcerer triggered the spell to react to our fears, and if you tell someone the manor is haunted, your fear will be... "

"Ghosts," Bray said.

"Naturally," Varthstone replied. "Except I don't fear ghosts. Part of my talents lie in dismissing spirits and poltergeists. So the illusion targeted what I was afraid of. Something that had nothing to do with an estate possessed full of vengeful spirits."

"But she broke the window."

Lotul shook his head. "You did. With your hammer. The illusion made you think it was her."

Aodhfin still wasn't sure. He had seen something before they opened the door, by the balustrades. Then when he had seen Esme's spirit, she was wearing the same chemise as she had worn when she murdered Gallach. Bray hadn't known that at the time. Still he picked out something important Lotul mentioned. "You said a sorcerer laid the trap."

"Yes," he replied, his hazel eyes sparkling. "And thus far we only have one in this town, don't we?"

Bray bit his lip at he thought about it. Who had the most motive to kill Gallach? "Fem Fonzil."

"The images we saw," Varthstone continued. "They were altered."

Bray shot him a look. "What?" he hissed.

"I didn't want to say anything in front of the mortician and give away that I knew, but they most definitely were altered in some way. We need to find out why."

Aodhfin thought on those words as they stopped behind Sange. She held a lantern down towards the tall grave marker. "Ere lay Adjutant Vey Gallach, a man o' war, a man o' the Maker," she said, reading his epitaph.

"Do you think Fem Fonzil lied about the key?" Aodhfin asked the sorcerer.

Lotul shrugged, "I suspect we will find out soon enough."

~ ~ ~

Between the three of them, they had the grave dug up in relatively quick order. Sweat and soil clung to him, making Bray's clothing feel like damp, soggy flesh. He was thigh deep in cold earthborn waters, and Sange, who was next to him, had ditched the shovel and was using her large hands to keep the running mud and clay at bay from sliding back into the hole.

"The casket is going to weigh a ton," Varthstone remarked. "Best to crack it and just remove the body."

"I'm not going to desecrate this man's final resting place any more than I have to!" Bray snapped. "This is bad enough as it is."

Lotul shrugged. "Have it your way, priest."

"All we have ta do is loosen it from da earth. Shoulda rise wit the water, right?" Sange asked.

"No," Varthstone commented from above them. "I took a look at the caskets while we were at the mortician's. Fem Fonzil weights them with stone so they will sink. I'm telling you, you'll need to remove the body."

Bray had a twisted feeling in his gut. "Well, Ser?" Sange asked. "What do ye wanna do?"

It was the first time in the last two days that she had respected his position, and Bray knew why. This decision was important to him. Detrimental to *him*, not them. She understood that, respected that. It gave him strength and an appreciation of the exactor at that moment.

"We crack the casket," Bray said finally. "We have to get that key."

~ ~ ~

Bray leveraged the shovel right between the slats, and Sange did likewise on the other side. "Ready?" he asked.

The woman nodded.

"Now!"

The two pulled their shovels with all their strength. Aodhfin saw deep grooves and valleys of muscles cut across Sange's forearm's and biceps. He was impressed in the details of her musculature. This was a woman who not afraid to be who she was.

It was against most of what the church stood for. Bray understood that. Ironic really, since the foundation of their faith was based on a woman's sacrifice. Still, Bray found himself respecting her usefulness.

Suddenly he felt a shudder in the handle of the shovel and it loosened considerably. A series of bubbles churned at the water they stood in, and then Bray felt something brush up against his legs.

A second later, a swollen body wrapped in cloth surfaced between the two of them. Bray looked down at it, confused, and then up to Sange. She had the same perplexed expression on her face.

He looked to the waterlogged body once more. It wasn't Gallach. In fact, it wasn't even human. Between the two of them floated a goat.

DECEPTION

"Is that a goat?" Varthstone asked, casting his lantern light into the hole.

"Yes it's a damn goat!" Bray growled.

Quickly, he pulled himself out of the hole. Sange followed. "We've been duped."

The sorcerer nodded. "Fem Fonzil."

Bray looked in the distance to where he knew the funeral home lay waiting. "It makes sense. Too much sense," he agreed. "Fem was angry. Not just with Gallach, but with Esme. She had deceived him, wronged him. He doesn't care about the will, or Gallach's possessions. He only cared that he loved her, and she used him."

"Then what are we waiting for?" Varthstone said darkly. "Let's bring him to justice!"

Bray nodded.

"Ugh... guys?" Sange interrupted. "I think we have a problem."

Sange pointed towards the entrance from where they had come. Standing there in the shadows cast by the gate was a lone, robed figure. A deep cowl covered their head, hiding their features. It stood there, watching them, unmoving.

"Fonzil?" Bray asked, reaching for the hammer at his waist.

Varthstone glowered at the lone figure. "I say we find out. Nothing I hate more than being made a fool."

Without waiting for Aodhfin's command, the sorcerer ran at the entity."Dammit, Lotul! No!" Aodhfin yelled after the Elf, but he did not turn around.

"What'n asshat," Sange remarked, drawing her axe in a single smooth motion from her back. "What do we do, Bray?"

"Flank it," Aodhfin answered immediately. "If it is a sorcerer, it will have a harder time with two separate targets."

Sange nodded and began to move left around the headstones. Bray went right.

Aodhfin kept his eyes on the unmoving figure as Varthstone ran towards it. When the sorcerer was only two dozen steps from the unknown person, it suddenly flared to life.

The cape flew open wide and three oblong objects scattered out with it. They took flight into the air, upon insect's wings, and it suddenly sounded like the graveyard was full of angry bees.

A small figure remained in the wake of the transformation. It raised a hand at the approaching Elf, and Aodhfin could only watch as the night turned to day before his eyes.

A huge fireball erupted directly in front of Lotul and, unable to slow his momentum, the unfortunate Elf vanished within the burning hot flames. There were no cries of pain, or screams of agony. Lotul was just... gone.

Aodhfin didn't have time to dwell on it as the three strange creatures flew their way. When they got closer to the separated duo, Aodhfin felt sick to his stomach at the sight of them. They looked like winged heads.

Aodhfin grabbed the shield off his back and rolled it forward with his free hand. In his peripheral vision, he could see Sange dropping her lantern and taking up her axe with both hands. The threat had just become very real.

They swept around the duo quickly, like hornets testing the range of their prey. Burning viridian flames flickered in place of their eyes and a series of barbed tendrils undulated beneath their wings like multiple stingers.

Aodhfin, no stranger to battle, kept his shield up and close to his chest, able to guard his exposed head if need be. He hadn't thought to wear his platemail in the graveyard this evening. He hadn't thought he'd need it. How wrong he'd been.

Sange swung her axe in tight, skilled strokes, trying to keep the winged monsters at bay. She did a good job keeping them back, but he knew the technique would wear her out quickly.

Aodhfin quickly looked back to where Varthstone had been. A large burning ball of fire stayed there, rolling in place. The small person, whom had been within the cloak, still stood by the gate, its features mute and indecipherable from this distance. Whoever they were, their focus was on the rippling globe of flames.

One of the creatures darted in at Bray. He raised his shield, deflecting a staggered series of blows from the stingers. A white pus-like substance dotted the surface of his shield, and it carried with it a pungent odor of decay. Like rotting vegetables.

Bray returned with his hammer, but the critter was too fast and easily avoided his blow.

Sange, across from him, was forced to fight two. She moved deftly for her size, maneuvering the woodsman's axe in a series of spins and twirls that he would have never thought possible from the weapon. It was like an extension of her being and she wielded it with the same finesse as a tigress used her own claws.

The winged beast moved in on Bray again, and this time the purist initiated the engagement. It came at him with a staccato-like attack, and as it swooped in,

Bray swung out with his shield. It bashed the thing across its deformed face, crushing what looked like a nose and drawing black fluid from its mutilated orifice.

Sange too, cut a sharp arc with her axe, severing a wing from one of the things and causing it to spiral out of control until it collided into a headstone with a sickening crunch.

The beasts withdrew, and Bray saw from the corner of his eye that they had drawn the attention of the sorcerer. He had little time to call out to Sange before their assailer directed the ball of fire at them.

Aodhfin saw the ball roll at great speed towards the warrior woman. Before he could even second-guess himself, he sprinted towards her. Sange watched, stunned, as the rolling globe of fiery death tore her way.

Aodhfin gave everything he had to get to her, and had it not been for the fact that the sorcerer had to navigate the ball around grave markers, he would have never made it. As it was, he beat the undulating conflagration only half a breath before it hit. He slammed into the blaze, shield first, forcing the fire to explode in a series of sparks that washed up and over the duo. Aodhfin felt the bite of the fire against his forearm. He smelled the sizzle of his cooking flesh, and felt the tightening of his skin, but he willed the pain from his mind until the inferno had subsided.

In its wake, everything around him, including his shield, was blackened and marred.

Aodhfin glanced at Sange, who looked at him in awe for only a moment. He flashed a quick smile, but felt it melt from his face the moment her doe brown eyes changed from awe to horror.

Bray spun and raised his shield just as a series of stingers rained down on him.

His shield took the brunt of the blows, but a single barb slid through and grazed his arm. Immediately it became heavy and numb and Aodhfin saw, more than felt, his shield arm drop to his side and the shield tumble to the earth. He stared at his limp arm, baffled as to why it didn't function, when he felt Sange's strong grip pull him back.

More stingers lanced through the air, and Sange thrust Bray behind her as the two remaining creatures swarmed atop her. She swung and weaved the axe in a miraculous display of skill, but it wasn't enough to stop all of the lashing barbs from poking through.

Bray watched in horror as Sange was perforated over a dozen times, white fluid running from the holes in her leathers and skin. Her axe fell to the ground as she dropped to her knees.

Aodhfin came forward, swinging his hammer in wild strokes trying to keep the monsters at bay, keep them away from Sange. He smashed one across the side, collapsing its body inward, and it spun away wildly into the distance. He looked for the other when he felt a sudden piercing pain in his back. His war-hammer slid from his grip, and then he was falling. In the distance, he could see the shrouded figure walking away, triumphant.

Aodhfin and Sange were on their knees, bodies numb and uncontrollable. They were face to face, only a foot a part.

"Aodhfin," Sange mumbled, her voice slurred from the toxins running rampant through her body.

"Be brave," Bray whispered, his voice equally drawling.

The sound of the beating wings flared around them. An echo of death.

Her brown eyes blazed. "I'm not afraid," she slurred.

The flurry of sound stopped, and the purist knew that one of them was about to die. He tried to look for it but lacked the strength to see where it was. Sange stared fiercely into his eyes.

"Pray fer me, priest," she whispered, and Aodhfin could only watch helplessly as her head disappeared in a flurry of wings and tentacles.

REVEAL

Sange did not scream.

Aodhfin began to pray aloud, his voice slurred and garbled, but he prayed. The mountainous woman's body writhed and twitched as the spurs drove themselves into her neck. The creature's whole body enshrouded her head, like a python devouring its prey.

Aodhfin continued to pray, growing louder even as his voice wavered. He tried to move, tried to fight the paralysis, but there was nothing. His limbs betrayed him. So he forced himself to watch. He would honor her. He prayed so she could hear him, all the way until her last moments, and he continued to pray even as her body stopped thrashing and fell still.

The tentacles pushed deeper into her flesh, and then Aodhfin heard a loud pop. Violently the creature pulled free, and Sange collapsed to the side.

Her head was gone.

The prayer left his lips. Bray still couldn't move.

Fear, oppressive and heavy, like water-laden armor, weighed upon him. A set of menacing eyes looked at him victoriously. They wracked his body with terror as they came closer, eyes that burned with an unholy green flame.

Bray wanted to raise his shield in defense. He wanted to pray to the Maker for his chosen deity's courage and blessings. He wanted to run. But he couldn't.

Paralyzed, and with all-consuming dread, he watched, helpless as it drifted towards him. A revolting, distorted head, suspended from insect-like wings. Around its ominous gaze was a crown of writhing tentacles all capped with wicked, barbed spines. Bray could see a pus-like fluid oozing from each of the dozen or so spurs.

The monster's mouth opened. He heard a loud pop and watched in disbelief as its jaws distended wide enough that it could enclose its maw completely around his own head. Jagged teeth slavered at the impending kill, and Aodhfin Bray knew without a doubt that he was doomed.

Therefore, he did the only thing he could. He closed his eyes and tried to tell himself to be as brave as Sange.

He waited to feel the pain thrust into his neck. He waited to feel the weight of the hideous beast close around his head. He waited to die.

The fluttering wings resonated in his ears like the beating of a hundred drums. It was a thunderous boom as it closed in on him. He knew the moment was upon him. His only regret out of all of this was that he never had a chance to tell Simonis about his son.

Even though the bishop was clearly a dishonest and immoral man, Bray wasn't. He should have told the man about his son. He had deserved to know. Now it was something that could never be.

He felt pressure then, but no pain. Surprisingly it was cold, as if the temperature around him had suddenly dropped. It was not something he had expected from a creature whose eyes emanated green flames.

Then he heard a thud, and felt something press against his numb thighs. Bray opened his eyes.

The creature lay there, against him, a lance of ice almost a foot long protruding completely through its head.

Confused, Bray looked up into the night. There, swaying, disorientated, through the forest of tombstones, steam rolling from his blackened robes, was Varthstone.

The sorcerer collapsed next to him, and immediately Aodhfin could see that some of the burns were quite extensive. Angry red flesh lined his face, and most of his blonde hair had been burned away. Blisters were already beginning to form on the Elf's hands, making using them difficult.

"Can you move?" he asked, his voice hoarse.

"No."

"Sange?" Varthstone said as he moved towards her. Aodhfin could only watch as he stopped halfway. "Oh, Sange."

"You need to go after Fem Fonzil," Aodhfin told the exactor. "You need to stop this."

Varthstone shook his head. "Not without you," he commented. "My arrogance already cost us Sange. I won't be responsible for you, too."

Aodhfin shook his head. "Don't blame…"

Lotul raised his hand. "Not now."

Aodhfin felt pressure on his body as the sorcerer began to search his wounds. "I think I can draw the venom out of you," he told Bray. "But it is going to involve magic, and it is going to hurt. Do you trust me?"

"Do I have a choice?"

"Not really," the sorcerer commented.

"Then do it," Bray ordered.

Varthstone swayed to his feet, placed one hand on Bray's back and began to draw on the magic of Creation. At first, the purist felt nothing but a strange budding pressure inside of him, then it began to intensify. Soon he felt searing heat and began to feel his blood boil. Pain ignited within him like an explosion, ripping through every fiber of his being and into his soul.

Aodhfin Bray screamed.

~ ~ ~

Minutes later the duo staggered to the funeral home. Bray had his shield across his back, but his hammer was in hand. Every nerve ending in his body felt like it was on fire, but he could move, and right now, that was what he needed.

Aodhfin hammered into the door, taking it from its hinges. It fell to the ground with a loud thud. They were now past the point of discretion. They knew there was very little time.

They moved with purpose, clearing each room together before moving to the next. Finally, they entered the back room where the scrying table was.

"No, no, no!" Varthstone said as he came around the table.

Aodhfin could already see that the surface that had once shimmered with glyphs was flat and dull. "It's gone."

Lotul slammed his fist against the table, and then hissed in pain as one of his blisters ruptured. He looked up, defeated. "We're too late."

Aodhfin let out a deep breath. He reached up and rubbed the locket around his neck in thought. As he did he saw a momentary flicker behind Lotul's head. Bray tilted his head as he stared, and then he saw it again. A gleam.

"What?" Varthstone said.

Bray moved around the scrying table and to the back of the wall. He studied it for a moment until he saw the shine of a glyph against a portrait.

"You've got to be shitting me," Varthstone said.

"Can you use this?" Aodhfin asked, nodding to the table.

"Damn right I can," he replied with a smile.

~ ~ ~

Fem Fonzil looked up at them through the table. "Purist, if you are seeing this, then I am dead," he stated bluntly. "Don't bother looking for my body as I'm sure they've ditched it somewhere by now.

"The image I showed you was modified. I figured it out shortly after you left because the inconsistencies bothered me. I missed things the first time because I'd been appalled by what happened. What I am about to show you are the real events that transpired. Brace yourself."

The image faded for a moment and then once more they were looking into the master bedroom of Esme. Everything played out the same as before, with Murrough entering the room and then the two caught by Gallach. After the beating of Murrough, and Esme's pleading, she went for the dagger.

She drew it on the elder man. Her stance was hardly threatening, and she looked awkward and unaccustomed to holding the weapon. Very different from the woman Aodhfin had seen murdering Gallach in the image, hours before.

Gallach moved on her with the skill of a seasoned veteran. In a single, deft move, Gallach wrenched Esme's wrist and plucked the weapon from her hand.

"That's new," Varthstone remarked.

This time the image didn't fade, and now he knew why. The creatures from the graveyard suddenly appeared from underneath the glyph.

"The fireplace," Bray murmured.

They swarmed atop the engaged duo and stunned them each. Both people froze in place. The creatures then disappeared the same way they had appeared, and Murrough entered the room.

He was fast and efficient as he pulled the dagger from Gallach's hand, sheathed it, and then scooped up Esme and carried her away.

The two stared at the image as Gallach stood there, terror in his eyes. Finally, Esme walked back into the room holding the dagger in her hands. Her back was to the glyph, but he recognized the chemise that she wore.

"This makes no damn sense," Varthstone whispered.

She straightened herself, adjusted her chemise once more, and fell into a combat stance that seemed far too natural to her compared to what they had seen seconds before. Esme lunged at Gallach. Apparently, the older man had gotten a little of his motor reflexes back, because he attempted to block the dagger. But it was too feeble, and Esme plunged the weapon skillfully into his right thigh. Gallach moaned in agony, but did little to stop her. She twisted the weapon and yanked it free, sidestepping the gout of blood that erupted with it.

The same slaughter they had seen before ensued, and then as Gallach lay bleeding out on the floor Esme turned to face the glyph, only it wasn't Esme, it was Nayria.

Aodhfin stared in shock. He now realized why she looked so familiar to him. Nayria looked like a younger, more slender version of Esme.

"Mother fu…," Varthstone said, fading.

She walked out of the room. Moments later Murrough came back into the image, holding Esme. He dropped her on the floor and left.

The rest played out the same, with Esme crawling into the blood, confused, tracking bloody handprints everywhere, and then screaming and dropping to the body. Murrough came in and arrested her.

The image faded back to Fem Fonzil.

"That's what really happened," he said bitterly. "Clearly I was wrong. Nayria *did* know about my glyphs, and she turned it to her advantage. She created a witness in me to prove Esme was guilty, just in case they needed it. Obviously until you came, they hadn't. Nayria knows I now know. I'm going to try to run, but I doubt I'll make it far, not with Murrough involved. I don't know why they did this, but you were right, the will is the key. You need to find it before they do. They never thought to look in the cathedral until I said something to you. I hope you had luck in retrieving the body of Gallach and that you now have the key. If I never see you again, good luck. And if I am dead, don't mourn for me. This has been a long time coming."

The image faded.

Varthstone looked up from the table to Bray. "Think he's being level?"

Bray shook his head. "I don't know. I still don't understand a reason here. Fonzil I get, Simonis I get, and Esme I even understand." He looked down at the reflective surface beneath them. "But Murrough?"

Aodhfin saw the patronizing look that Varthstone was giving him. "Give me a motive," he demanded and pointed to the table. "That was planned, Varthstone. Premeditated. I want to know why!"

Varthstone's expression changed. Slowly he shook his head. "I don't know why Murrough would be involved. We don't know him, don't know his history with Gallach. Perhaps he was like Fonzil, and found out he wasn't Esme's only lover."

Aodhfin grunted and waved a dismissive hand at the sorcerer.

"I'm trying to give you a reason, you stubborn son of a bitch," the Elf snapped. "This image is far more convincing to me than the last one we saw. If Fem Fonzil is lying, this one is a lot better than his last. If he's not, well he's now dead. So justice prevails there, eh? Nevertheless, you need to look past the fact that he's an adjutant, Bray. You are not infallible, you are human."

It was a hard reality for Aodhfin to face, but Sange had said almost the same words. They were only human. It was a similar realization as when he had watched Barodin die. The invincibility of youth had been lost in the wake of a dead friend. Perhaps it was time he shed his ignorance as well.

He acquiesced with a nod.

Varthstone clasped his shoulder gently. "I know it's not easy," he said with more empathy than the Elf had used in the past. "Now there is only the matter of getting into that abandoned church. If there are truly the wards Fonzil spoke of, then we still need a key."

A key.

A thought began to swirl in Aodhfin's mind. When they had needed to breach buildings before on the field of battle they had used a gnomish device called a 'master key'. It would propel a concentrated charge into a door, breaking locks and destroying barricades.

"Could you create a key, or tear down the wards?" Aodhfin asked.

The sorcerer shook his head. "That's not really my forte," he admitted.

Aodhfin nodded. He found his fingers on the locket, stroking the hasp that kept it shut. Even though locked, he knew with the right amount of force he could open it, even crack it if he wanted.

"I have a plan," the Purist said.

"A plan?" Lotul replied. "That fast."

Aodhfin shrugged, "More like part of a plan."

Varthstone crossed his arms. "Well then let's hear it."

Aodhfin explained.

MASTER KEY

Varthstone held up the rolled up piece of parchment in his hands. "This is crazy, you know that?"

"Will it work though?" Aodhfin asked.

The sorcerer grinned. "Oh, it'll work all right."

"Good, then we both have jobs to do. Good luck," Bray said.

Varthstone nodded as they left the funeral home. "You too, Bray. Be careful, and don't die."

With that, the sorcerer ran off into the night and towards the docks. Aodhfin knew they were thin on time, and he only hoped he wasn't going to be too late. He headed back to the graveyard.

When he arrived it didn't take him long to search for what he was after. He picked up the grotesque creature and examined it quickly. Underneath the strange disembodied head, he found two thick, leathery sacs. When he squeezed one he watched some of the stingers emit the white fluid. Carefully, he cut away one of the sacs and the attached tendrils. Very gingerly, he put it in his medical sack. He then looked up at the old cathedral.

This close to it, the ancient edifice looked imposing. It wasn't often that a church of the old gods remained intact. Most were torn down when the five-spired cathedrals of the Enclave were constructed. Gallach must have fought to keep it from sharing a similar fate.

Just inside, he could see the dancing light of torches, and he knew that it must be Nayria and Murrough. Now he needed to give them the sign.

Aodhfin searched Sange and found her flask of oil and flint. It need not be big, Aodhfin knew, but he wanted to make a statement. He dumped the entire flask on the front of his shield and struck the flint against the metal. Immediately the entire face of the shield erupted into flames. He shouldered the burning barrier and waved it high above his head.

Aodhfin looked out into the Sowle Sea and saw a returning glint of light. The purist drew his hammer and looked down once more at the remains of Sange. "I think you would have loved this. This is for you, girl," he whispered, and he charged the church.

~ ~ ~

A hundred feet from the towering double doors of the antique structure, Bray heard the sweet sound of thunder in the night.

A series of three booms all back to back. It was about to storm. It wasn't nature that was calling, but the Maker. Aodhfin had his master key.

A shrill whistle cut through the air as Aodhfin caught the quickest glimpse of it tearing through the darkness. It struck the side of the age-old building, rocking its very foundation, and tearing a massive hole through brick and wood.

The second whistle hissed by and Aodhfin saw as his key slammed into the earth, creating a two-foot-wide divot, and then bounced into the double doors. The primordial wood shattered under the might of the cannonball, tearing one down completely and swinging the other wide.

The third ball slammed through one of the stained glass windows and caused untold damages within.

Phase one complete. He only hoped that Varthstone was on the move, because now it was Bray's turn.

Aodhfin charged into the church, launching over the broken timber easily. His flaming shield lit his way, but he knew that it wouldn't last much longer. That was fine. His message was delivered.

The inside of the church was a mess of vegetation. Between the cracks of the foundations, vines had found their way inside and thrived. He saw vermin skittering away, terrified to have their home disturbed after so long.

He had little time to admire the antediluvian architecture and instead searched for the murderers. He needed to find them and stop them before they got the will.

Bray pushed past debris and stone pews as he worked his way to the back chambers, and to the last place he had seen light. The west end. He made his way there.

The purist ducked under a deteriorating arch just as he heard the crunch of rubble. He spun just in time to see the flash of his firelight reflected off a silvery blade. He raised his shield, deflecting the blow and bringing him face to face with Adjutant Murrough.

~ ~ ~

"Who in the hells do you think you are?" the veteran growled as his blue eyes flared with hatred.

He pushed Bray back and moved forward in a series of concentrated stabs meant to drive Bray to ground. Aodhfin, however, had fought Wilders, and he was used to the overpowering might of their attacks. Murrough, in contrast, was a much smaller man.

The purist deflected all the attacks skillfully between his shield and the head of his hammer. He returned in kind with a low swing hoping to take out the adjutant's knee. Murrough narrowly avoided the attack.

"Not bad, boy," he commented dryly as he came in high with another series of tightly-controlled swings, forcing Aodhfin to be on the defensive. "But I have time and experience on you."

Bray didn't answer as he deflected the incoming attacks. He let Murrough get close before he suddenly lashed forward with his shield, bashing the adjutant in his shoulder and causing the man to stumble backwards.

The impact took out the last of the fire in an explosion of sparks. The room grew dim, only illuminated by the starlight from outside.

Aodhfin felt his skin begin to tingle, and looked down at his arm in surprise as the hairs began to stand on end. He felt pressure building in the air around him. Knowing what was coming next, he dove into a roll just as a burst of light exploded behind him. He came up just in time to catch the brunt of the fulmination in his shield. Electricity discharged across his arms and drove through to the heels of his boots, chattering his teeth and stunning him. Aodhfin knew it could have been much worse though, had he not caught the bolt of lightning in his shield.

Nayria stepped into the starlight, looking every bit like Esme in the pale glow. He thought he understood then. "You're her daughter."

"Eldest daughter," the Manhym hissed. "Illegitimate, of course."

Bray's fingers and toes were numb from the electrical current that had poured through his body. He knew if he moved he would be sluggish and easy game for both Murrough and Nayria, so he stalled. "But why?" he demanded.

"Because I was denied!" the woman hissed. "No one could know that I was Esme's love child, begotten out of marriage. It would destroy Gallach, and no one could have that!"

Bray glanced to his left and saw Murrough stalking in the shadows. Trying to flank him, Nayria continued. "Gallach was a hero back then, and when he went on one particularly lengthy crusade, my mother had a dalliance with an Elf. The result: me. Bishop Simonis managed to keep it all secret, saying that Esme was terribly sick and bedridden at the estate. There, he cared for her, and delivered me. I was taken away to be raised in an orphanage while my 'sister' lived a life of luxuries. Three winters ago I came back to find who my parents were, and I learned the truth!"

Bray nodded at Murrough. "From him?"

She scoffed at him. "I need only look in a mirror, purist."

Aodhfin felt his strength returning right as Murrough charged at him. He ducked the man's viscous slash and punched out with the shield, catching the man in the ribs as he passed.

Murrough grunted and tumbled past him, crashing into a stone pew.

Nayria lashed out with another arc of lightning. Bray raised his shield in defense, but was too slow; the bolt ripped the battered shield from his hand, stinging it viciously.

The sorceress stepped forward, her fingers extended at Bray, and he knew she had him. "Where is the will!" she demanded.

Aodhfin looked up at her, baffled. He then realized that they hadn't found it yet. Quickly his mind modified his plan. "It's safe," he lied.

She came forward and gripped his throat. He felt the trickle of electricity dancing across her fingertips, biting into his neck. "I will kill you," she spat.

"And it won't bring you any closer to the will," he answered. "You are running out of time, Nayria. You have hours left before Simonis takes it all. Then where will you be? Same as before, an orphan with no family."

Her green eyes were livid. "Oh I have family, purist," she remarked darkly. "And I think it's about time that you met them."

ENDGAME

Murrough regained composure quickly and took Aodhfin's weapon away from him. At sword point, he was forced to follow Nayria down into the catacombs. She grabbed a torch off the sconce and led him through a series of passages. As she did, she continued explaining how she learned of her patronage.

"When I arrived, that slime, Bishop Simonis, immediately became infatuated with me. I was naïve and childish, and had dreams of finding parents that loved me. In return for... favors." Bray watched her gag, revolted at the memory. "He told me the truth about Esme. It was a hope beyond my wildest dreams."

Bray could hear the longing in her voice, but watched as her face turned twisted and dark. "I approached her, her long lost daughter, and what did she do? Rejected me!" she spat. "Cursed me, told me I was a liar, and a sinner, and a foul creation and to get out of her life and never return! My mother!" she laughed bitterly.

"I tried everything to make her love me, but all she ever loved, all she ever needed, was the infatuations of men." Her eyes were cold and ruthless, just as Aodhfin had seen Esme's in the image when she had slapped Gallach. "I even tried blackmail, but she had the backing of Simonis, and he quashed that, threatening to have me tattooed and branded for having intercourse out of wedlock. The monster."

"I was lost, until Murrough found me," she said, glancing back to the man. "He knew of Fem Fonzil and his dalliance with Esme. He knew the Elf was a sorcerer. He conspired to have the mortician train me in the art of **Creation**."

"Why?" Bray blurted. "What was in this for you? An adjutant of the Maker! How could you?"

Murrough looked at him, his blue eyes so dark they seemed indigo. "The Maker," he spat. "This life has taken everything from me. My wants and desires. My hopes and dreams. The woman I wanted to be with was too lowborn for a purist, so they sent me here, leagues away from her where she could marry someone of rightful station. Then they shipped me a rightful bride." He scoffed. "A sow of a woman who was so bitter she could make milk curdle. She wanted nothing to do with me. She didn't even try to love me. Instead, she demanded that I care for her like Gallach 'cared' for his wife.

"I cared for her alright." The way he said it left no room for interpretation.

"When I met Nayria I thought I had a chance for something real again. But even that was spit upon because she is lowborn. Well she won't be when she is declared living heir of Gallach, will she?"

Aodhfin could see Nayria's white teeth glistening in the torchlight. She held her head high as she walked him into a wide circular room.

"You'll never guess who I bumped into when we came to the cathedral this evening. Hiding here all this time. I should've thanked Fem Fonzil before I killed him."

Another one of the beasts was there and the sight of it made Aodhfin cringe. It hovered, green eyes alight with flame. Tentacles undulated in the air. All of its tentacles but one. He followed it down and stared wide-eyed at the slumped over form before him.

"This is my sister," the Manhym told him. "Say hello to Daria."

~ ~ ~

"Now this is how I see it," the dark-haired Manhym said as she paced around Aodhfin. "A purist will never give in to torture, right? You'd resist until I had no choice but to kill you. It is your way, after all."

She turned away from him and walked up to the slumped-over woman. Nayria grabbed her by her shoulder-length brown hair and yanked her head back violently. Daria was only a young girl, perhaps fifteen winters at most.

Immediately one of the creature's spurs came around and stabbed into Daria's neck. The girl twitched. Aodhfin tried to lunge at them, but stopped when he felt the length of Murrough's sword at his throat.

"That is what I thought," Nayria said with a smile. "You will do anything to defend an innocent, won't you?"

Aodhfin glared at her, outraged. "You would kill her for... for wealth?"

Nayria nodded. "And love," she added, looking at Murrough. "The question is why will you let her die? What is in this for you, purist? The murder has already been solved. No one questions it. Your job is done here. No one at the Citadel cares about Sentinel's Barrow. Why do you care who gets Gallach's wealth? I mean look at your choices: a corrupt bishop, a heretic who turned her back on the Maker, or an orphan. Really, is it such a hard decision?"

"When the orphan is a murdering psychopath, yes. Yes it is," Bray fired back.

Nayria's eyes darkened. "Funny. I didn't think purists had a sense of humor."

Another stinger slammed into Daria's neck and she started to gurgle.

"Oh. Look at that," Nayria said flatly.

Aodhfin took a deep breath, his body quivering in rage.

"The will," she demanded.

Bray tilted his head. "Have you checked Gallach?"

"His body was the first thing I eviscerated. There was so little of him left in the mortuary that I had to place a goat in the coffin to give it weight," she hissed. He had forgotten that she was the mortician's assistant.

Bray flinched as another spur buried into the girl. Daria let out a strained moan.

"I'll tell you what. I'll let you think on it, but don't think long." The tentacles rolled in Daria's neck causing her body to convulse. "The Vaus'Giel is impatient for its meal. The more impatient it gets, the harder it is to control."

Aodhfin knew he was out of time. He could see the Vaus'Giel's mouth slavering in anticipation, and he would not let Daria die. Nayria was correct in her assumption of his character, he couldn't abide it. He let his hand fall under his medical pouch.

"Okay," he said, hanging his head low.

Nayria's eyes widened in expectation. "Where?"

Aodhfin looked down and began to open the medical pouch with his other hand. Seeing this, Murrough knocked his hand out of the way and thrust his hand inside.

Bray squeezed the bottom of the pouch gently.

Instantly Murrough recoiled his hand, hissing in pain. He turned his hand over and he stared at his palm in shock. Four tiny perforations were on the pad, all oozing a white, pus-like fluid.

Aodhfin felt the sword at his neck droop, and he reacted.

He plucked the weapon from Murrough's hand easily, just as the Vaus'Giel dislodged itself from Daria. It came at him in a flurry. Prepared, Aodhfin swung the sword in perfect precision as it arced towards him, tentacles writhing.

Moving on its own momentum, the creature couldn't avoid Bray's attack. Its face exploded in a mist of black cruor as the sharp blade cleaved through flesh and bone, cutting it in gold.

Nayria screamed in rage.

Aodhfin grabbed the paralyzed Murrough by the shoulder and spun the man in front of him just as the sorceress attacked.

Lightning cut through the air like a deadly knife. It lanced forward with lethal speed, headlong into the frozen adjutant.

The veteran grunted in pain as the fulguration hit him full bore, crashing through his chest and exploding out his back. The force of the attack knocked Bray back.

"No!" Nayria wailed in horror as her dead lover collapsed to the floor, a smoking fist-sized hole in his chest.

Aodhfin crinkled his nose at the scent of burned flesh. He moved on Nayria while she was still in shock, raising the borrowed weapon up to the sorceress' chest. "It's over."

Nayria spit at him, "I'd rather die! You'll nev…" She never had a chance to finish. Aodhfin turned the sword to the flat of its blade and backhanded her across the face with the weapon. He couldn't risk her casting any of her perfidious magic after all…

Nayria crumpled to the ground, unconscious.

~ ~ ~

An hour later, the local militia was escorting a bound and gagged Nayria out of the catacombs. Daria was now conscious, but groggy. She had taken a heavy dose of the Vaus'Giel's venom.

Varthstone made sure that she received care, while local healers doted on him as well.

Bray had to admit: the exactor had really come through. The Elf's task had been to conscript the captain of the ship they had sailed on to blow a hole in the cathedral. Sange's death sealed the deal.

Afterwards, he had to force Bishop Simonis to go to the funeral home where he would have to bear witness to the true nature of Adjutant Gallach's death via the scrying table. Judging by the swelling around the bishop's left eye, Aodhfin felt that Varthstone may have 'forced' a bit too hard. That was fine with him.

Aodhfin now found himself alone with Bishop Simonis. "I supposed congratulations are in order, Purist Grey," the thick-bodied man said condescendingly. "But I don't see why this couldn't have waited to be brought to my attention until the morning! You have everything under control here."

Aodhfin took a deep breath. It was all he could do to keep from striking the man. Instead, he pointed his finger into the obese man's chest. "You are partly responsible for all of this!" he growled at the bishop. "Your blatant disregard for the lives of those around you, whom you are supposed to serve, is a mockery to the very church you represent! You are a sinner, a tyrant, and a fraud. I just wanted to tell you this in person before I give my full accounting of what transpired here to Adjutant Daz."

"How dare you, Grey! You have no right to speak to a man of the Maker in such a way!" the Bishop bellowed.

Aodhfin grabbed the collar of the bishop's vestments and pulled him close. "It's Bray! And I have every right!" he hissed. "You abandoned the values of the Maker a long time ago, you piece of shite! If it weren't for my love of my friend Barodin, I would strike you down right now! It'd be doing this world a favor."

"Speaking of which...," Bray began. As much as he detested the man, he had a right to know. A right to know about the fate of his son. He let go of the bishop and unclasped the locket. He placed it in that elder's soft hand. "I regret to inform you that Purist Commander Barodin H. Simonis was killed in action defending the Citadel against insurgents on the third day of this season of greening."

For a moment, Bray thought his voice might fail him, that he wouldn't be able to convey the message, but it had not. Still the anguish of his own words poured from him. The persistent hopefulness of his human heart had refused to let him accept the intuitive certainty of his friend's death. He had been there after all. He had seen it. Now, though, in conveying it to the bastard before him, the reality came down hard.

He felt his own eyes watering.

The bishop looked down at the locket. "My son is dead?" he whispered.

Bray nodded.

For the first time, the bishop appeared human to him, weak, as his face turned purple in what Aodhfin knew was an inescapable sorrow filling every part of him. "But why the locket?" Simonis asked, his voice faint.

"I don't know," Aodhfin admitted. "Adjutant Daz gave it to me before I set sail for Sentinel's Barrow. I had assumed it was a personal article of Barodin's for you."

"Actually it belonged to my father," a wisp of a woman's voice said between the two.

Aodhfin looked down to see the rundown frame of Daria standing near them. "May I?" she asked holding out a shaky hand.

Simonis, lost in grief, didn't even recognize that he was handing the locket to a heretic. He dropped it in her hand absently.

Aodhfin, who had been tempted to open the locket repeatedly, watched as Daria reached down and deftly undid the latch on the side. When she opened it up, he saw clearly the drawn likenesses of Daria and Esme inside.

Then Daria did something most curious. She turned the locket over and slammed it between her palms. Suddenly the little drawing popped out and Aodhfin could see it was part of a larger piece of parchment, meticulously folded.

"When my father was killed, I knew immediately that it had not been my mother. Still, Murrough closed the case and executed my mother before anyone would even begin to investigate. I knew no one here would listen to a girl who had turned from the Maker, over an adjutant who had witnessed the whole 'murder'. I needed an outsider. So, I sent this locket along with a note to my father's old friend, Adjutant Daz, pleading for aide. I also knew that whoever killed my parents must be after their wealth, and that I was the only connection to that wealth, minus the will. So I hid where I knew no one would care to look and I put the will in the safest hands I knew of."

She unfolded the parchment repeatedly until it was almost the size of her hands. Aodhfin could clearly read the very first line: 'The last will and testament of Vey Gallach'.

She smiled up at him. "The hands of a purist."

Aodhfin couldn't help it; he began to laugh.

EPILOGUE

Adjutant Daz looked over his desk at Purist Bray with concerned eyes. "I had no idea the malfeasance ran so deeply."

Bray nodded. He had just finished explaining in full detail his accounting of the Sentinel's Barrow murders.

Suirokirt Daz took a deep breath and placed the written report on his desk. "You did a fine job, Aodhfin. I didn't mean to make your first command so perplexing, but you handled it well, very well."

"Thank you, Ser," Bray said.

"I hope you now understand why I assigned Exactors instead of Purists for this case?"

Bray nodded. "You needed impartial parties. Too many Purists, and we would have sided with the Church without question."

The adjutant nodded. "You have a sharp wit Aodhfin, and an open mind when necessary. For that I am glad."

Daz slid another parchment across his desk. "In fact, you handled yourself so admirably against a sorceress that I think this next assignment should go to you."

Bray looked down at the words scrawled atop the docket, 'Ambrosia'.

"Do you feel up to it?" Daz asked.

Aodhfin nodded. "Yes, Ser."

"And how do you feel about magic, son?"

Aodhfin looked out of the office where he saw his exactor waiting. He turned his head and looked Daz in the eyes. "After what I've seen, after how I was manipulated by an illusion, after watching comrades die to beasts under a spell, I think it is perfidious and vile."

"I see," Daz said.

Aodhfin continued, "But I also think in the right hands, those tempered by the Maker, **Creation** can be a gift."

"And you think Exactor Varthstone is such a man?"

Bray nodded. "I think he can be, yes."

"Good to know."

"Your daughter, too," Aodhfin added quickly. He remembered that Daz's daughter is a gifted healer and didn't want to sound too disdainful towards magic users.

"Yes... my daughter," the adjutant replied absently at his words. Almost distantly.

Bray saw something peculiar in Daz's eyes, so he knew he should quickly change the subject. He looked down at the words before him once more. "I must admit that I found the betrayals in the church more troubling than any of the magic, Ser."

Aodhfin glanced up to see a tired look now in the adjutant's eyes. "The closer we are to the light, the darker a shadow we cast, my son. Temptations of the forbidden can be strong if not tempered by faith, friends, and family." He looked down sadly. "Sometimes we cast that shadow deeply onto the ones we love, instead. We suffocate them in a void so black, and we don't even realize we are doing it."

"Is that what happened with Esme?" he asked.

Daz shrugged. "I don't know," he answered and pinched the bridge of his nose. "Perhaps."

A long silence filled between them. Bray found himself waiting uncomfortably. Finally Aodhfin thought Daz was done speaking about it and was about to conclude their briefing when he suddenly continued. "Sometimes I think our struggles as men of the Maker push our women away from us. We lose sight of how precious they really are. How fragile our connection with them is. Then they do something completely irrational, that makes no sense whatsoever, and forces us to realize the demons of our own ignorance. Like a cry for help that is heard far too late."

Aodhfin could see Daz's eyes watering as he looked out of the window of his office towards the monolithic spirals of the Citadel.

"You think Esme had made that cry once?"

"I think she made it many times, and they fell silent against our deaf ears."

His tone of voice, though, and his use of the word 'our' sounded very different to Aodhfin, as if it were more personal. "Ser, is something wrong?"

A tear broke away from Daz's dark eye and cut a swath down his rugged face. "My Carmella," he whispered.

Aodhfin felt his stomach drop and his body grow cold. "Your daughter," he said quietly. 'My Carmella', echoed in his mind. His beautiful, radiant, intelligent, fifteen-winter-old girl. A young woman engaged to be wed to a purist she hadn't seen in over a winter.

Daz's eyes looked to Bray apologetically.

"She's pregnant, Aodhfin."

THE PURVEYOR

Golden eyes followed their prey.

She hopped merrily across the field, oblivious to the danger that she was in. She rifled at the ground searching for a patch of green grass amid the yellow thatch. All the while, he moved closer.

The young girl looked up swiftly, her expression like that of a confused rabbit. He froze. If he were to be victorious, his stealth was of the utmost importance.

Her downy light brown hair fanned out in the breeze like a flag. It billowed there as she searched for agonizing seconds.

Ten seconds.

Twenty seconds.

Did she see him? Did she know he was here?

The small child returned to the ground once more, searching for another suitable patch of fresh soil in which to plant her flowers.

He made his move. Quickly, he rushed forward on all fours, slinking through mounds of black hardened clay and tall thickets of yellowing grass.

The oblivious girl moved away at a leisurely pace, but he knew he didn't have much time. He needed to strike. Now.

As silent as a whisper he sped up to just behind her.

He pounced.

Strong legs propelled him through the air, and he collided into her would-be attacker's back. His arms and legs wrapped around the creature and brought it to the ground. A dagger glinted in the dull light, and he drove the weapon down against the creature's neck. There was a pop, and the creature was no more.

Swiftly and silently, he dragged it into hiding. Once more he froze as the little rabbit-like girl pitched her head to the air and looked around in confusion. She could feel what happened. The attack. It was on the very air. She sensed that something was very wrong. The child bolted away, suddenly terrified, and in moments was gone.

She was safe.

Rhall the Spriggan stood up out of the thicket. Rabbit-girl would never know how close to death she had come. He glanced up at the deeply overcast clouds in the sky and then down to the still remains of the shadow creature that almost killed her.

The Purists called them ursers. Evil minions of the Rhacotis sorcerers. Hunters of life using the dark places.

The spriggan looked down at the small leather pouch he kept at his waist. He reached inside and drew another dagger, small, and forged of metalline blue steel. A weapon made to fight against evil.

He reached down and finished the deed, assuring the urser would never threaten anyone again.

Curious. Why was this creature so far removed from its desert home? More to the point, why was it in Halsbren?

Those were questions Rhall needed answers too. There was an unauthorized Sorcerer in Halsbren, and it needed to be dealt with, quickly.

THE URSER

Rhall travelled discreetly across the green bluffs on his way north towards the dark hillock that was Halsbren Proper, the capital of the small nation of Halsbren. In his mind, the teachings of the Purists danced through his head, helping to preoccupy his time. It was a nice distraction, though he himself was not a Purist. To be a Purist one needed to be an elf or a human.

Rhall was a spriggan. Compared to many races, he was considered incredibly small. He averaged the same height as that of a small human child. His skin was beige and his frame was petite, like the lithe form of an elf. Large pointed ears stuck out from underneath thick brown plumes. Not truly plumes as many people thought, but quills like a porcupine's, which lay recumbent against his head unless threatened.

Also uncommon to many of the other races were his prehensile tail and claws. All of these he kept hidden, more so for the sake of the fearful humans than his own peace of mind. Rhall was not ashamed of who he was or his race.

He kept claws were long and sharp, and he was dutifully trained by many masters on how to use them effectively. He was taught to stalk silently in the shadows, to hunt, and to track his prey.

To kill his prey.

And his prey was…evil.

He was an Exactor.

He didn't come into the trade by upbringing or through any kind of tutorage. He came from a different walk of life. At one point they might attach the word criminal to his name. Not anymore.

Rhall knew his job as an Exactor was the Jasian Enclave's necessary evil. His duty was to complete the missions that the Church could not and would not openly admit to doing. He was expendable, and he loved it.

Everyone in the church knew that he and others like him existed, and yet their presence was rarely seen, only felt. Purists, adjutants, and the occasional bishop were the people that directly connected with Rhall and his mercenary ilk.

Not every mission for him was about murder and deceit. But his skill sets did loom more in that direction than most. He heard rumors that other Exactors were more flexible.

Currently his mission was simple but violent. Kill all errant sorcerers that threatened the nation of Gurgen and its vassals. Lately those rules extended north of Gurgen to their allied neighbor, Halsbren.

While Halsbren's laws allowed for Sorcerers, it was still Rhall's job to eliminate any and all that posed a threat to the Jasian Enclave.

Rhall liked his job. He was very good at it. Small things that bothered other people, things like blood and entrails, didn't bother him. Moral delineations between right and wrong were for the weak-minded, not for the logical and the efficient. And Rhall was nothing if not efficient.

He tightened the cloak around his shoulders as he moved. The temperature was still very cold. Cold did bother him. Especially when it came on suddenly.

Two brutal storms hit Halsbren back to back; blizzards that pounded from the northwestern mountains with several feet of snow. Snow storms like these often claimed at least one life. It was only a matter of time before he heard word; the farmer caught in a field, a stable master trying to save his flock, an elderly woman not making it home from the markets in time, or the poor family who hadn't wood in their hearth and froze huddled together. There was always one tragic tale.

Rhall's gaze drifted skyward. Dark clouds kept the sun firmly at bay. It wasn't unusual for the sun to be gone for so long in Halsbren, but he didn't care for the lack of warmth in this nation, or the dimness of the light. His prey though... It was everything the ursers embraced. Cold desert nights, and starless, lightless skies.

Yet why follow the storms? Such darkness could not last forever, and then the urser would be vulnerable. Logically it didn't make sense. Something was clearly afoot.

Rhall's first impulse after stopping the urser was to find the nearest Purist contingent. So, he did. If anyone knew about trouble brewing it would be them.

The Purist's outpost was about a mile north of the small township of Ost Farhuud. It was a half a day's walk from his 'hunting grounds', and as he crested the horizon line that showed him the hewn stone walls of surrounding a lone tower, he knew something was wrong.

Alarm coursed through him as he closed the distance. He could not see a single venerable member of the Jasian Enclave standing guard at the open portcullis, nor any visible sentries amongst its walls.

He crossed the worn threshold into the circular den that normally housed a contingent of Purists. Only biting cold and howling wind greeted him. The outpost was vacant.

Concern sliced through him deeper than the bitter winter wind.

A quick survey showed no signs of conflict. Not a hint of a struggle. It just seemed abandoned.

A new problem. Another piece added to the puzzle. Logically he should pursue this thread as finding out what happened to the Purists was likely garner the quickest results. If he did that though, it would leave others at the mercy of the ursers. He thought of rabbit-girl. If he went in further search of the Purists now, ursers might kill her, or any like her.

Rhall was only one person. So that meant one problem at a time. His true objective was to find the source of the ursers. He would have to solve this anomaly later, if he could. Rhall set out to track the ursers on his own, fully knowing the dangers he was heading into.

~ ~ ~

His stalwart ally, logic, told him that the best place to stage an attack was the Halswood. A forest that lay nestled between the deserts of Malten and the neutral kingdom of Halsbren. If ever someone wanted to launch a campaign against Halsbren Proper, the Halswood was it. It wasn't exactly a welcoming spot, but logic never considered comfort in its equation.

The ursers were a threat to life in Halsbren. They could be stopped, killed, and even banished back to the Nether plane, sure, but most simple folk were unaware of that.

Rhall could appeal to the king himself. The Kingdom of Halsbren was no stranger to the arcane. The contained their own bevy of sorcerers, the Court Mages, and they were under the direction of the king himself. But even then, they were small in number and could not be everywhere if the threat of the ursers spread.

No, time was not his ally in this. Rhall needed to find the ursers' base of command before they infested basements, catacombs, and dark alleyways. Before they became a scourge. He needed to find and kill the sorcerer that controlled them.

This was Rhall's saving grace. Controlling them was far from easy. The sorcerer needed a focal urser. An alpha. That meant they needed to keep it contained and hidden. Like a queen in a hive. The best way to do that was the caves in the Halswood.

There was nothing light about the Halswood. They were dark and foreboding. Underneath the canopy, they were thick with thieves and creatures of ill-repute. Few safely ventured within. Less returned.

If any unregistered sorcery was happening, especially from a Maltenese sorcerer, it would be there. He took a deep breath, summoned his courage, and set out to do what an Exactor was meant to do.

Exact punishment.

HALSWOOD

It took three days to reach the outskirts of the Halswood. Rhall stood at the top of a small cliff right on the forest's edge, where he found the strangest markings.

All around in a half circle at the edge of the cliff looked like scorch marks on the ground. They were blackened silhouettes in the earth and looked to be a few days old at most. He looked at dark brands upon the patchy land carefully. Very, very faintly he could make out the slightest of impressions. They were tracks that came from within the forest to this edge. Someone discovered something they shouldn't have and paid the price. Sorcerer perhaps? He eyed the blackened marks again. It looked that way.

In any event, their failure was his gain as they left clear depressions upon the ground that he could follow back into the woods and, hopefully, to the sorcerer. There was only one way to find out. And Rhall was determined to do so. He stepped into the Halswood.

~ ~ ~

Many residents of Halsbren Proper would whisper that the Halswood was a place of nightmares. Deep within the forest, the trees were so close together that the canopy of branches above interwove like skeletal fingers, creating one long, seamless wooden ceiling. This caused the forest itself to loom with darkness and raised the creepy factor to boot-shaking, even in the late afternoon.

Rhall noticed immediately that everything was silent. Not a chirp of a bird or a peep from an insect could he hear within. There wasn't even the whistling of wind through the trees. It was like a forest of the dead.

Rhall's golden eyes fell to the trees. They were barren of any leaves thanks to the onset of winter. The branches were naked and frail, the bark a rich black.

The ground looked like nothing so much as a bog of frost and grime with small mounds of thorns growing here and there.

The entire forest was a place of gloom. Luckily, Rhall was prepared for such a sight, so what might have filled him with dread and despair was nullified by logical acceptance. He understood the fear though. He faced it, let the fear wash over him, through him, and pass on. As always, when it was gone, only he remained, strengthened by his inner resolve.

The spriggan travelled to the origin point of the tracks, deep within the foreboding woods. Rhall was alarmed to see not just one set of tracks now, but several.

One was from a four-legged creature, likely a dog from the paw prints he saw, and three other sets.

The dog and another headed in the direction of Halsbren Proper, while the other sets he followed ran back to the cliffs.

"They were decoys." Rhall whispered as he thought he understood. "Very brave." And so very dead.

This unfortunately answered his question on the disappearance of the Purist contingent. They came in force, likely reaching a similar conclusion as he to the whereabouts of the hidden sorcerer. Their fate though had not lasted. The scorched remains he saw on the cliff's edge were all that remained of that unit, minus whomever they protected with their decoy and sacrifice. The knowledge that the Purists were killed should have turned him away then and there. Instead if fueled him to continue.

Even in knowing the fate of the Purists, it didn't answer why the ursers were roaming the countryside. One might have escaped, but there was no way to be sure that they got away. He couldn't risk heading to Halsbren Proper to find out only to have more people suffer and die so he could gather a safer confirmation. Rhall went deeper into the Halswood than many ever dared.

He was aware as he went of the many eyes that were upon him. As silent as he may be, you could not hide from the shadows.

The spriggan only hoped to confuse and elude them long enough to find out why they were targeting the peoples of the countryside. He knew by the daylight that he did not have long before he would have to leave the forest. To camp within the darkness of the Halswood while being watched by ursers was not smart. It was suicidal.

Eventually Rhall came to a cave, and he knew he was at the right place. A darkness so oppressive greeted him. The entrance looked more like a wall of black than a hole cleft into rock. Only the shadow creatures could thrive in a place so dark.

Rhall was forced to make a choice. He could hope that the sorcerer was within and attempt to draw it out, or he could go in himself. Into the lair of the ursers and their potential master.

Rhall knelt down on the muddy turf and grabbed a piece of his cloak. With his sharp claws, he cut a good chunk of fabric away. He plucked up a decent sized branch and wrapped the cloth around it tight. The spriggan reached into the pouch he always kept at his waist and withdrew a small bottle. Amber liquid rolled back and forth within: oil.

He poured the contents onto the makeshift torch and then lit it by rubbing two sticks together hard and fast. Soon a lively orange fire burst to life on his branch. This would be his protection. In the darkness, ursers grew quickly frightened of sudden bright light. The only downside was that the sorcerer would know he was coming.

Rhall entered the dark cavern, very aware of the shadows unnaturally skittering away from his extended light. If he was going to find his answers, they would most certainly be here.

WHAT WE DO

The shadows slinked away from his movements as Rhall carefully walked deeper into the cave.

Was this their den? Did the shadow creatures make dens in the absence of a sorcerer? If so, he was in terrible danger, and yet his task would not let him be anywhere else.

He needed to find answers. He needed to know how to protect the people of the Halsbren against these creatures. He needed to kill a sorcerer.

Deeper and deeper he moved. The walls gently reflecting the amber light of his torch. It flickered wistfully in the windless corridor.

The ground was hard on the pads of his feet, the stone a bluish-black, like obsidian. In the distance, he could hear the echo of dripping water. His tongue tasted the condensation on the air, heavy with minerals.

Suddenly the narrow passage opened up before him, and he found himself in a large wide chamber. Stalagmites and stalactites jutted from the ground and ceiling, reminding Rhall of being in the mouth of a great stone beast. All around him, the shadows whirled and writhed, trying to attack him with their teeth and claws, but having to flee the light when they got too close.

Terror welled within Rhall. He wouldn't let it control him. He was close now. He could feel it.

Passing the rows of rock teeth, dripping sound grew louder. In the center of the chamber was a pool of water. Droplets rained from the ceiling into the growing pool. And in the center of that was a large mass of shadows.

The shadows twisted and spun, rolled and danced. Rhall went near it, and it suddenly wheeled on him.

A sinister voice echoed in the chamber, "Leeeeavvvveee thisssss placccceeeee fleesshhhhhh."

It spoke! Rhall realized. It must be the alpha. He wasn't aware that ursers were capable of words. He always assumed they were merely constructs, like golems. This was clearly not the case. They were intelligent!

"Where is the sorcerer that controls you?" he demanded.

"Ambrosssssiaaaaaa," it hissed. The glob of shadows rolled towards him like a massive black ball until it was right outside his immediate torchlight. "Symmbioounnn binds."

"Ambrosia?" Rhall said quietly. "Symbioun binds?"

He knew that name, Ambrosia. He heard it in whispers between the Purist Aodhfin Bray, and that of his master, Adjutant Daz. Ambrosia was a powerful beguiler that eluded the stalwart Purist of nigh seven winters. Was this was this one and the same? And what did it mean by Symbioun binds?

The beast lunged forward rolling up water from behind it. Rhall, momentarily distracted, cartwheeled away, but not before being doused in the water.

The flickering light of the fire died away. A blanket of total darkness covered him, and the surrounding shadows swelled.

"Oh no…"

~ ~ ~

A feminine laughter ripped through the darkness. Rhall tried to pinpoint it, but the acoustics of the cavern made it echo all around him.

"You should have left when it told you to, spriggan." Her voice cut into the void around him.

Rhall could feel the pressure of the ursers gathering around him like a vice.

"Are you Ambrosia?" he asked into the black.

Again, a feminine chortle rang out. "We are but little pieces to a much greater puzzle."

Rhall didn't like the sound of that at all. If it was Ambrosia, he needed to tell a Purist. He was outclassed here. He began to back up, but the cold pressure of the urser against his back stopped him hard.

"Why are you in Halsbren?" he asked, stalling for time. "Why are you hunting with ursers?"

The cold around him tightened, and he found little room to move. He knew he was trapped from his exit. His need for knowledge put him here. Perhaps a bit more sagacity on his part might have eliminated his current predicament. Damn that pesky logic. Then again, if he were one to use logic all the time, like most of his race, he wouldn't be an Exactor either.

"I'm paving the way," she told Rhall. His stomach dropped when he heard her next words. "And the mortar starts with your blood."

"Diiiiieeeeee!" The creature in the pool roared.

Rhall felt the shadows press down on him. Claws pressed towards his flesh. He scurried to the floor, the shadows toppling over him. Luckily for him, spriggans were small and wiry, and the shadows were thick masses and ungainly. The ursers swarmed on top in a monkey pile of pressure, cold, and claws.

Rhall rolled out of the pile of shadows and flipped away from their deadly attacks.

Black forms took the shape of flat faces. Within those faces, sharp fangs gnashed for his flesh. He heard hissing and sputtering from the sorceress to kill him, but Rhall did not stop. He ran.

He burst from the cave in a full sprint. He glanced back for only a moment to see a flood of shadows pour out after him, and behind them, he saw her. The sorceress.

"Crap" he whispered, and pushed himself harder.

Rhall wasn't a hardened battler as the Purists were. He could fight and defend himself when necessary, but he was no real warrior. He was an assassin, pure and simple. He had no way to defeat so many shadow beasts, but that wasn't his purpose. She was.

So Rhall kept running. He knew he needed to warn someone about Ambrosia. As Rhall ran his mind raced with him. Who was Ambrosia? How was this sorceress 'paving the way?' And what did the shadow beast mean by Symbioun binds?

He saw the creatures gaining ground on him, and with a cold dawning of reality, he knew that he wouldn't be able to escape them. Like the others, there would be no escape for this spriggan.

The creatures drew even nearer. A glance backward showed him a wall of shadows, fangs, and awaiting death. They howled, growled, and clawed for Rhall.

His mind reeled. If he could make it back to the edge of the cliff where he found the blackened remains, maybe he could make his way down and increase the gap between him and the ursers. Maybe, just maybe, he might have a snowball's chance in the hells.

His instincts screamed that was the smart thing, the logical thing, for a spriggan to do. But this sorceress, Ambrosia, or not, was a threat to Halsbren right now. She was a threat to everyone.

And she controlled the ursers...

The ursers were on his heels. He felt their cold pressure on his back. He was seconds away from his flesh being torn from his body. His chance of escape was so minimal it was almost worth laughing at. Even though Rhall knew the logic of still trying to escape, he knew his odds were long. He was a dead spriggan. That left only one cold, hard option left. Complete the mission.

Rhall spun and redirected his path back through the forest. The wave of shadows, caught off guard by such a dramatic directional shift, tumbled forth clumsily in pursuit, granting him a distance of a few seconds. He reached into his pouch and drew his dagger. It burned a strong metallic blue in the light.

He had one shot. To do the unexpected.

In a wide circle, he put everything into the run. His small legs trucked hard as he kept the ursers just at bay. The entrance of the cave came back into view, only from a new angle.

The sorceress was still facing the direction he ran off in. She was confident that his pursuers would kill him. And she was probably right. But if he stopped her here, the ursers would fade back into the nether. Not right away. Not before they ripped him to shreds, but before they could hurt anyone else. Before they could harm any more children.

He squatted as low as he dared as he bolted forward towards her left flank. She remained oblivious to him up until the last ten feet.

She turned as she saw him from the corner of her eye. Rhall roared and lunged into the air, blue tinted dagger leading.

The sorceress reacted on impulse, she flung her hands before her, and Rhall watched as dust instantly coalesced around her open hands creating three razor sharp shards of ebony stone. Airborne, the spriggan could take no cover, no defense. The sorceress released the shards with lethal speed.

Instinct forced him to twist in the air as best as he could. He watched as one shard flew by narrowly missing his face. A second whizzed behind him, rippling the cloak across his back. Wood splintered and exploded outward from the edge of a nearby tree as the sharp obsidian shards ripped through it, as if it had no more consistency than wet paper.

Rhall wondered what happened to the third shard when he felt an explosive pain in his right arm. It sent his twist into a wild spin that crashed him hard against the packed dirt.

Agony like lightning arced up his arm through his shoulder and spread throughout his body like a spider's web. He looked down at his wounded appendage only to see in shock that his entire hand was gone, as was a portion of his wrist.

Blood pumped furiously from the tattered meat, and two white shards of bone protruded, jagged and sharp.

The sorceress laughed once more as he stare helpless at his rent weapon hand.

"Futile, foolish little creature." She barked, "You should have fled when you had the chance."

Rhall felt her hands around his throat jarring him from his shock at losing his hand. He gasped as she squeezed down on his delicate throat.

Even though she was a human woman, her size still tripled his, and her hands went completely around his neck. She held him rigid, choking the life from him.

"I don't need magic to kill you, vermin," she hissed at him.

Rhall gasped and gagged as she squeezed and squeezed. This was it. End of the line.

Darkness began to line the corners of his sight. He felt his heart rate slowing down. His body sagged.

"Don't close your eyes, rodent," the sorceress commanded. "I want to watch your life leave them."

And she leaned close to him. Her green eyes bore into his golden ones. Their noses were almost touching she was so near, staring so intently for that moment when his eyes went glassy and distant.

Rhall saw then, reflected in her green eyes, not his own death, but opportunity. He felt her forearms grazing against his plumes.

In a final surge of adrenaline, he willed his plumes to flare to life ripping deep red trenches against the sorceress's mocha skin.

She screamed in surprise and pain. She let go, but he gave no quarter. He didn't wait until he had a breath in his body, he pressed.

He slammed his head into the sorceress's face. Her scream turned into a gurgle as his quills pierced her forehead, cheeks, chin, throat, and eyes.

He ripped backward with a grotesque suctioning sound, and then slammed his head into hers once more for good measure. She collapsed to the ground at his feet, her face a mass of hemorrhaging holes.

Blood bubbled out of a perforation in her torn throat and ran in rivulets from the frenzied punctures across her face. One green eye was decimated. All that remained was a glob of oozing yellowish pulp.

She looked up at Rhall, a wet, pained sound escaping her lips. Then her head fell backward and she went still.

Rhall collapsed to his knees, in his own pain and exhaustion. He did it. He stopped the sorceress. Stopped Ambrosia.

A wall of shadow loomed up behind him. Knowing he was at his end, he didn't bother to look up. "Just do it," he said.

He felt the cold hard pressure of the urser touch against his back. Rhall cringed, it was going to hurt, but he was spent. There was nothing left.

"Weeeeeee arrrreeeeee freeeee," it croaked above him. "Shheeeee isss gonneee."

Rhall nodded. "Ambrosia is dead."

There was a rough grating sound like two stones rubbing against one and other, and Rhall realized the urser was laughing at him. He risked looking up at the deep rolling shadow before him. He growled, "You mock me in the end?"

Slowly it answered, "Sshheeee isss nottt Ammmbbroosssiaaa."

Rhall groaned, and forced himself to his feet to face the dark creature.

It held up a single claw and pointed north. "Shheee issss inn theeee Wilddssss."

"The Wilds," Rhall whispered to himself. That was why Purist Bray had never been able to find her. She was with the Wilder people in a land so fierce, so terrifying, none would dare venture.

Rhall looked to the urser. "Are you going to kill me?"

Deep soulless pits for eyes stared back at him. "Noooo," it answered, and then pointed at the sorceress. "Weeee arreeee gooingg tooo killlll heerr."

As if understanding what was happening the sorceress began to stir. She opened her one good eye and stared up at Rhall and the wall of shadows behind him.

Her mouth opened in horrid recognition of one simple fact. She no longer had control of the ursers.

"Go ahead," Rhall agreed. "I have everything I need here."

Rhall wrapped the cloak around his mangled arm and walked towards the ursers. They slowly twisted out of his way and turned on the fallen sorceress.

Rhall didn't give them a second thought. He knew as well as they that without the sorceress binding them to the mundane plane they would soon fade back to the nether. Their time was short, and justice needed to be met.

He heard the ursers swarm the sorceress, and he didn't care. Nor did he care when he heard them violently eviscerate her flesh, tearing her slowly to pieces. Nor did it bother him when he heard her agonized screams, as she was rent limb from limb.

After all, murder didn't bother Rhall. Not under the right pretenses at least. She brought this upon herself. And the same fate would befall next sorceress who got out of line.

He wasn't sure he would survive the walk to Halsbren Proper, but he knew he had to try. A message need to be sent to Adjutant Daz and to Purist Bray. It was time justice was finally met to one of the most elusive beguilers of them all.

Ambrosia.

Turn the page for a preview of:

A BLOOD WIZARD CHRONICLES
NOVELLA

RAID

Screams echoed throughout the hillside as Stormwind and Carmella ran to the outskirts of Agot. Carmella yelled for Militär first, and then Rosethorn, but her voice was lost in the din of all the others. People were panic-stricken, running wildly away from the massive lumbering forms that moved between buildings.

Stormwind grabbed the arm of a woman fleeing away in fright. She wheeled on him, swinging and screaming crazily. "Whoa, whoa!" he said as he blocked her attacks. "What's happening? Who's attacking Agot?"

Terror-glazed eyes barely looked at him, only flickering to what lay beyond. "The Wilds," she muttered. "They came from the Wild lands."

Stormwind let go of the woman and let her join the throngs of other terrified townsfolk making their way toward the Order of the Sacred Fist for protection.

He looked between the escaping men and women, trying to eye their attackers. The Wild lands to the south of Agot were an almost forbidden territory. Most trade companies preferred going around the long string of mountains to the southeast. They would rather add scores of days to their journey than to risk the rolling aureate plains of the Wild lands. Creatures of disturbing size and foul ilk brooded within the serene-looking landscape.

Those vile things that lurked within the Wild lands, however, lent strength to the few foolish enough to live within. Men and women held fortified towns within the plains, surviving against all odds. Over the generations it caused the peoples within to change. Like the hard and feral monsters of the land, the men and women, too, became hard and feral. They became fearsome and barbaric, their stature in most cases rising to well over seven feet in height. These hardened peoples relished in the fight, in the violence of survival, and in the victory of life. They were often known as Wild Men, or simply Wilders, and few were ever seen outside of the borders of the Wild lands. If they were, it was often as trackers or mercenaries.

The clash of metal on metal sounded nearby bringing Stormwind out of his thoughts. He looked over in the direction of the noise. The ringing of steel against steel was rhythmic to him, almost soothing. Stormwind felt himself drawn to it. He drew his ornate rapier in a smooth motion and stepped forward. To his surprise, Carmella followed fearlessly by his side, her eyes ripping across the townscape looking desperately for her son and friend.

They rounded the corner to look into the alleyway beyond. Four men were engaged in mortal combat. It was three against one. Two of the men were the Agot guard, one a monk, and the other was indeed a Wild Man.

The Wilder towered over the others, casting them in his shadow. He was at least seven feet tall and almost three feet wide at the shoulders. He wore virtually no armor, nor clothing, instead wearing only the skins and furs of the monsters of the Wilds on his body. Stormwind could make out what looked like

Sabertooth Tiger skulls on the massive man's hands, and the skin of a reptile, perhaps alligator, running over the barbarian's knees and feet. His thighs, chest, and arms were bare, showing thick, hardened muscles and a myriad of scars that were bred from countless battles. His face was hidden behind the visage of a basilisk's skull, a terrible lizard that dwelt within the Wild lands. It was said that the beast could kill by its very breath, or even with a look, and this man was wearing it's skull as a trophy. A testament to his skill in combat.

The Wild Man handled the trio of men easily, swinging his cumbersome great axe with ruthless efficiency. The man overmatched the guards before they even engaged him. Within seconds the two were cut down, their life's blood pumping hot spray against the walls of the nearby structures. The Wilder fought through the crimson mire without any regard for having taken the men's lives.

The monk, however, fought on. His skill and speed were an exemplification to the teachings of the Order of the Sacred Fist. The monk dodged the axe blows easily, maneuvering quickly between the openings the Wild Man created, to strike him in a flurry of ruthless efficiency. As Stormwind ran to his aid, he could already see welts forming across the barbarian's body where the monk had struck home. Still the monk's crushing blows did not seem to faze the barbarian in the slightest; if anything, the Wild Man seemed to fight even harder.

Stormwind managed to reach the monk's side just as the giant axe whistled through the air for his head. The nimble Elf deftly avoided the blow and struck with the speed of a cobra, plunging the thin blade up between the Wilder's ribs and piercing his heart.

Hazel eyes stared through the gruesome mask, perplexed. Stormwind understood, for he had seen the look before. The barbarian knew something was wrong, yet he felt only a pinch. Stormwind twisted the blade, opening the wound, and then yanked the sword back, removing it from the giant man's chest. Instantly the Wild Man's bewildered gaze went wide in shock and he fell to his side, dead.

Stormwind turned to the monk. "Quickly . . ." he began, but was halted. Also crumpled on the ground was the monk who had been fighting so hard. The great cleave that Stormwind had narrowly avoided had not missed the monk. It had struck true, removing the warrior priest's head from his shoulders. Stormwind felt the bile rise in his throat at the sight of the dismembered head lying only a few scant feet from the body. He turned away. There he saw Carmella staring in agony at the dead monk. She had likely known the man.

The High Elf reached gently toward her and took her olive-skinned hand. "Come on Carmella," he said quietly. "There's nothing we can do. Let's find your son."

The words brought Carmella's gaze away from her fallen compatriot. She nodded to him and said not a single word. Then they were off travelling deeper into Agot, and closer to the heart of violence.

~ ~ ~

They arrived in the market place where Stormwind had first met Carmella only two weeks before. The tables and chairs were now turned over, and it looked as if many townsfolk had barricaded themselves within the tavern. Outside, the Agot Militia fought valiantly against the overwhelming size of the enemy. Everywhere Stormwind looked, the men and even women of both the Order and Agot were fighting for their lives against the monstrous Wild Men.

Like the one that Stormwind had encountered in the alley, many of the other barbarian men were covered in the hides and furs of their conquests as well as the skulls of their triumphant victories. Some of those skulls were even humanoid.

Stormwind rushed into the fray with Carmella close behind. He fought with speed and precision and with a deft agility that even the Wild Men were not prepared for. Within moments, three of the barbarians lay dead at his feet and he prepared to advance on more. Behind him he could hear Carmella screaming for her son within the tavern. No one answered her and Stormwind feared that he knew why: Militär was not there.

Stormwind lined himself up with other members of the militia. "Do any of you know Rosethorn?" he yelled to them as they held back the advance of three more Wilders. The barbarians were learning to fear the sting of his blade and were now more reluctant to recklessly advance on him like before.

"Freckled girl?" one of the guards yelled back behind the overturned table. Stormwind tried to maneuver towards the one who had called out the vague acknowledgement but the Wild Men barred his way.

"Yes," he yelled instead. "Have you seen her?"

A Wild Man roared at Stormwind and swung his axe down to cut the Elf in half. Spittle flew from the gargantuan mouth, flinging outward like small moist projectiles. Stormwind sidestepped both. He leapt into the air and drove his rapier down between the man's clavicle and neck. The blade parted the soft flesh easily and sunk low, piercing multiple organs as it passed through his body. Stormwind removed the sword in the blink of an eye and landed gracefully back on his feet, all in a single fluid motion. The Wilder gurgled as he collapsed to the ground.

The remaining militia killed the other two barbarians and shortly after, the soldier came out from behind the table. "I tried to get her to come into the tavern, but she wouldn't listen."

Carmella, hearing the conversation ran up to Stormwind's side. "Did she have anyone with her, a small child perhaps?"

The soldier nodded. "Aye that she did. 'Fraid she wouldn't listen to me. She headed that way," he finished as he pointed east.

Stormwind looked in the direction the soldier indicated, perplexed. "But that's further away from the monastery. Would she not be trying to get to protection? Wouldn't she be trying to get Militär back to you?" he asked as he looked to Carmella.

"I don't know. She is probably just scared. Stormwind, we have to hurry! Rosethorn is not a monk, she is a local. She does not know how to defend herself. And Militär . . ."

Stormwind nodded; he understood. Rosethorn could walk right into a Wild Man ambush and not even see it coming. She would have no way to protect Militär then. He grabbed Carmella's hand, squeezed it once reassuringly, and then headed east through the ravaged town of Agot. Buildings were scarred with the deaths of so many. Blood graffitied the walls wherever they went and bodies littered the streets.

However, it was not a total massacre; far from it. The militia could be heard holding their ground, and for every two Agot corpses they found, they found one Wild Man. The barbarians were taking casualties, too. It was only a matter of time before the Wilders would have to declare the battle a rout and withdraw. Stormwind did not think Rosethorn and Militär had that kind of time though.

They looked in every house they passed by and Carmella would call out to the two of them. Still he had not heard a response from either. Nevertheless, one thing he did notice was that they were encountering the Wilders far less frequently. It looked as if the eastern end of the town had been the first to feel the effects of the raid and now the core of the Wild Man advance had held firm in the center of town. It made it easier to search for Carmella's son, and if Militär were around, he would find him.

The two reached the edge of town. Beyond, all that Stormwind could see were farms and tilled fields. If Rosethorn and Militär were cutting through the farmland, Stormwind's keen elven sight would be able to see them but as it was, there was no one to be found. Everyone that was not fighting had fled to the monastery to the west. He turned and looked to the woman whose child he was trying to save. "Did Rosethorn know the farmers well? Would she take Militär to a barn perhaps?" he asked, and then turned to look at the tracks on the ground.

He already knew the answer before she said anything, though. Fresh tracks were only coming in; none were leaving. The tracks inward were also massive depressions that he had gathered came from the footfalls of the Wild Men. There was nothing so small that it denoted that it came from a child or a young woman. Still he waited for Carmella's answer.

"No," she remarked. "Perhaps we missed them somehow," she said with a reserve of calm Stormwind was amazed she had.

"They could have doubled back towards the monastery. Perhaps someone convinced Rosethorn to head there?"

The High Elf watched as the dark-haired beauty bit her lower lip in frustration. "Perhaps," she agreed.

Stormwind began to turn back when suddenly he saw a flicker of movement. The Elf reacted on impulse, pushing Carmella out of the way and diving to the side just as three shards of ebony stone tore through the wooden fencing that they had just been standing near.

Stormwind ended his dive in a roll and came to his feet, his ornate rapier ready. Carmella, however, was not as graceful when she hit the ground.

Stormwind's cerulean eyes scanned the cluster of houses behind him. Carmella and he had just looked in every one and they were empty. From where had the attack come? Then he saw it: the silhouette of a woman in a doorway some twenty feet away. How had he missed that? He heard a chanting sound as she raised her hands once more. Instinct forced him to spin away from her and around the corner of a nearby home. Brick and mortar exploded outward from the edge of the house as another trio of sharp obsidian shards ripped through the building, as if it had no more consistency than wet paper.

He knew what it was then: Magic. The assailer was a sorceress of some kind.

"Krake, finish him," he heard a vaguely familiar voice say from around the corner.

Stormwind pushed himself up against the wall and slowly crouched. His gut told him that he should flank around the building and try to attack the assailers from behind, but as he glanced to Carmella lying prone on the ground he knew he could not leave her behind.

Then a large bone-plated leg stepped into his view of the fallen monk. Stormwind followed it upward to the largest human he had ever seen in his life.

The man had to be close to seven and a half feet tall, his shoulder span reaching almost four feet across. Thick heavy muscle rippled across the huge Wild Man's body through pockets of leather and fur that were patchworked amidst his towering frame. The skulls of basilisks resided on each shoulder, and his dark grey orbs stared down at Stormwind through the skull of an armor-plated crown of a gorgon. Two long horns rose off on both sides of the skull and jutted forward like hooked javelins. Stormwind could see a tangled black beard sticking out from beneath the gorgon mask.

"You must be Krake," he said dryly as the Wild Man roared at him and swung a colossal poleaxe with both hands. The agile Elf easily rolled away from the hulking monstrosity of a man before him and came to his feet once more almost six feet away.

Krake spun around instantly, rolling the poleaxe around easily with the skill of a master. Stormwind looked at the long weapon with a well of fear growing in the pit of his stomach. The poleaxe was over six feet in length with an axe head, a haft of a hammer, and spike tip across the top. It was a versatile weapon and one that hindered the Elf. The barbarian had range and size on Stormwind, and the Elf needed to be close to be effective.

Krake swung the poleaxe in a wide arc, Stormwind barely managing to duck out of the way of the curved blade, when the immense warrior instantly followed through with a crushing slam of his hammer. Stormwind narrowly escaped the pulverizing attack as the hammer head slammed into the cobblestone road, shattering the smooth stones into fragmented slivers and dust.

Stormwind attempted to gain his footing but the Wild Man vigorously advanced. The Elf backpedaled frantically as axe fall followed a swing of a hammer, followed by the stab of the spear tip. It was as if there was no escaping the overpowering goliath. Finally, the deft Elf managed to flip over a small fence to grant him a modicum of room before the Wilder shattered it, too, with a swing of the hammer. Stormwind could not believe the man's speed and endurance for his size. It seemed inhuman!

The Wilder pushed forward, confidence gleaming in his dark glare as he forced Stormwind into retreat again and again. Stormwind thought for sure that the

Wild Man was invincible, when he made his first mistake. As he stabbed forward, he kept the hammerhead facing his opponent and the axe away. Stormwind realized the strategy, for if the Elf dodged to the outside, as the Wilder expected, he could follow through with a sweep attack from the axe, effectively hamstringing the Elf. Stormwind was not going to give him the luxury. When the piece came forward again, instead of dodging to the side, he moved forward.

He spun wide letting the sharp spike slide along the inside of his armor. As he came around he caught the hammer haft and used it as leverage to hurtle himself forward. Within the Wild Man's perimeter and against the weapon, the massive man was defenseless. With all his strength, he stabbed forward. His thin blade perforated the seams of the Wilder's muscled flesh and drove completely through his body, erupting in a crimson explosion as the tip exited his back.

To Stormwind's surprise, the Wild Man did not so much as grunt. Instead, with amazing willpower, Krake dropped his poleaxe and instead grabbed Stormwind, who was so close to the goliath he could not escape in time.

Krake's hands locked onto Stormwind's shoulders, binding his arms in place. With unbelievable strength, he lifted Stormwind from the ground. The grip on his arms was excruciating. Stormwind tried to hold onto his rapier but found the lock on his arms too tight and felt his grip ripped away.

Stormwind knew that things had taken a turn for the worse, but still he did not relent. As the hulking monstrosity squeezed down on him, crushing the air from his lungs, the Elf kicked as hard as he could against the man's flank. If the Wild Man noticed at all, it did not even register. Krake lifted Stormwind up so that the Elf was looking through the eyeholes of the gorgon skull to the man underneath. It was a visage of death. He knew this was the end, yet he remained defiant. With all the power he could muster, he spit into the eyehole.

Krake drove the skull helmet down on Stormwind's head. Searing pain and bright light exploded all around and everything began spinning. He felt the crushing blow again and the light was now replaced with stars. Then he was falling.

The ground rushed up to greet him and he slammed down hard on his side with a cry of pain. The world spun and swerved before him and lights danced all around. He felt hot fluid pouring liberally across his head and down his face. He looked up at the monster above him.

Pain ran through his body like lightning, coursing from his neck down to his toes. Still he watched as the Wild Man slowly reached down to his own abdomen and removed Stormwind's rapier. He made no sound and Stormwind could only watch as the cruor-covered blade slid wetly from the barbarian's body. When the tip finally emerged, a red gout of blood followed it. It was then that Krake grunted. He put his hand over the crimson-drenched wound and threw Stormwind's rapier down.

The Elf tried to move, but his body would not respond. He could only watch as Krake picked up the poleaxe once more. He arced the axe head towards Stormwind's neck, and with one hand raised the weapon for a felling blow. The blade began to race downward.

"Wait!" a woman's voice called.

The blade stopped only inches from Stormwind's face. He stared at the glinting metal hovering so closely above him.

Suddenly a freckled female's hand came into view as she pushed the weapon away from his face. She bent over and smiled wickedly down at him, her green eyes glittering in triumph. "Well... well... well... what an unexpected surprise? And to think I thought it was actually the Agot Militia giving my Wilders such a hard time. I should have figured it to be a High Elf."

He watched helplessly as another Wild Man walked by with an unconscious Militär hanging limply from his shoulder. His gaze fell back to the woman as tears began to stream out of his eyes in shock. She stood up, "Goodbye, Stormwind."

~ ~ ~

Aodhfin Bray and Stormwind will return!
Continue their saga in the novel, The Blood Wizard
Chronicles: Stormwind, or check out any other exciting
works by Jay Erickson, available at Amazon.com,
CreateSpace.com, on Amazon Kindle, and at
www.AuthorJayErickson.com

If you enjoyed this novel, please take a moment
and review it favorably. Every bit helps.

Thank you.

Jay Erickson
Author

~~~

ABOUT THE AUTHOR

JAY ERICKSON grew up in Midwestern USA before joining the United States Air Force at the age of nineteen as an aircraft mechanic. In 2001, he separated from active service and became an Air Force Reservist.

Since that time, he has held a variety of jobs from working at a casino, to operating cranes, to laying brick. Even with a myriad of different careers, though, writing has been his primary interest and hobby. As an avid reader, he has always held a deep love for Fantasy and Science Fiction. It was a natural fit for his writing. Now he's taking that hobby one step further by joining Halsbren Publishing LLC and releasing his saga THE BLOOD WIZARD CHRONICLES for others to read. Mr. Erickson resides in Northwest Indiana with his wife and two children.

~ ~ ~

PRAISE FOR

Blood Wizard Chronicles Novella-Pononga

"Jay Erickson's writing is extraordinarily lucid and vivid. He entwines the story-line and the characters with uncanny detail and pragmatism, it makes you think you're truly watching Stormwind and his exploits! I found myself pondering what would happen next, and couldn't wait to get home from work to continue reading it! I highly recommend it!"
   -George Kramer, author of the *Arcadis Fantasy Series*

Blood Wizard Chronicles Novella-Dark Consort

"The character of Stormwind is aptly named, as he floats in to people's lives and shakes them up in more ways than one! The author weaves a complex tale marrying classic heroism and mystery elements with modern ideas in a complex fantasy world. Stormwind's character acts as a catalyst, moving the action and keeping the reader guessing as to what might come next. Follow Stormwind's path and get a deep and exciting look into the culture, intrigue, and emotions of a unique race of Elves through this new novella from Jay Erickson."
   -Anastasia Trekles, author of *Core*

"Jay Erickson spins a tale so engrossing it left me hungry for book 3 and thirsty to re-read book 1. An intriguing tale that maximizes characterization, instantly taking me into his world. Highest regards, you won't be disappointed."
   -C.E. Rocco author and Editor-in-Chief, Old School Publishing

Blood Wizard Chronicles Novella-Stormwind

"*Stormwind* is an intense, character-driven melodrama that never ceases to be entertaining. It's heroes are immediately likeable and the action is vivid, but it has just enough substance to make the reader think. Plus, it has so many plot twists both M. Night Shyamalan and Christopher Nolan are jealous!"

-Nathan Marchand, author of *Pandora's Box* and co-creator of *Children of the Wells*

Blood Wizard Chronicles-Pariah

"*Pariah* is a fine example of intricate world-building with an interesting take on the standard fantasy tropes. A complex tale featuring adult themes and intriguing, relatable characters, it's a promising beginning to the *Blood Wizard Chronicles* series."

-C.S. Marks, author of *The Elfhunter Series*

"Readers who expect serialized cliffhangers in each chapter, popularized by authors like Dan Brown, may be disappointed. Instead Jay Erickson builds every moment to an intense conclusion, using graphical landscapes that are vivid and provide the backdrop to a powerful dialogue that drives the story. The emotional and psychological depth given to the characters shows that Jay Erickson is laying the groundwork for a growing future with each interaction."

-Brad Mitchell, PhD, MA, MS, Med. Associate Professor of Psychology and author of *Surviving Psychology*